firefly

A TRAVELER'S COMPANION TO
THE 'VERSE

firefly

A TRAVELER'S COMPANION TO
THE 'VERSE

BY MARC SUMERAK

ILLUSTRATIONS BY LIVIO RAMONDELLI

INSIGHT EDITIONS

San Rafael, California

CONTENTS

A shepherd once told me a story.

He pointed out at the 'Verse and said that everythin' out there—every single speck of light in the gorramn black—was handcrafted by the one and only God himself.

I couldn't help but laugh. Not out of disrespect—no sir—but because a grown man ain't got much time for fairy tales. Even a bèn tian sheng de yi dui ròu like me knows where all of this came from and why it had to be made.

See, maybe the Almighty did create Earth-That-Was, but mankind went and destroyed it all on their lonesome without any divine intervention. That left 'em with a choice: to die on God's good Earth or to make themselves a whole new universe where they could keep on livin'—at least until they destroy this one, too.

And so, here we are. The 'Verse. A collection of dozens of planets and hundreds of moons, each one shaped by the people who live there and the challenges they face. The further you get away from the Core, the more you believe that God didn't bother to come along for the ride.

To be fair, though, I ain't never been one much for religiosity. Captain's job is to believe in two things and two things only—his ship and his crew. And thanks to them, I've had the fortune to see more worlds than most folk. But when I'm alone at the helm some nights and I look out into that silent void, I can't help but wonder if there ain't just a hint of truth to what the shepherd said.

The 'Verse may have been reshaped by man, but it was here before we were. And no matter how many maps you study or guides you read, there's no denyin' that it's bigger and more complex than any of us can ever hope to comprehend.

If there is a God out there, I ain't found him yet. But it's a mighty big 'Verse. Reckon I'll keep sailing this boat until I do, one way or another.

Malcolm Reynolds
Captain of Serenity

P.S. As you use this guide, keep a look out for notes from my crew—some helpful, some not so much. We've been all across the 'Verse and have seen the good, the bad, and the fèi wù. We don't got all the answers, but if you're reading this, well, clearly you ain't got 'em neither.

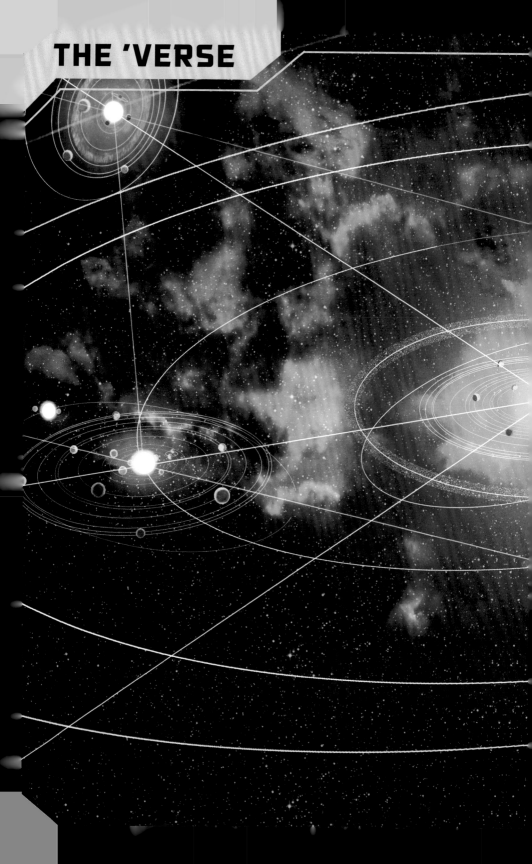

The term *universe* is used to describe the entirety of the cosmos, including all matter and the space between. The more colloquial term, *the 'Verse*, however, refers to the system in which all human life currently resides. Composed of five stars, seven protostars, and more than seventy planets and their corresponding moons, the worlds of this system are as diverse as the people who dwell upon them.

But the cows look the same no matter where you go. —Wash

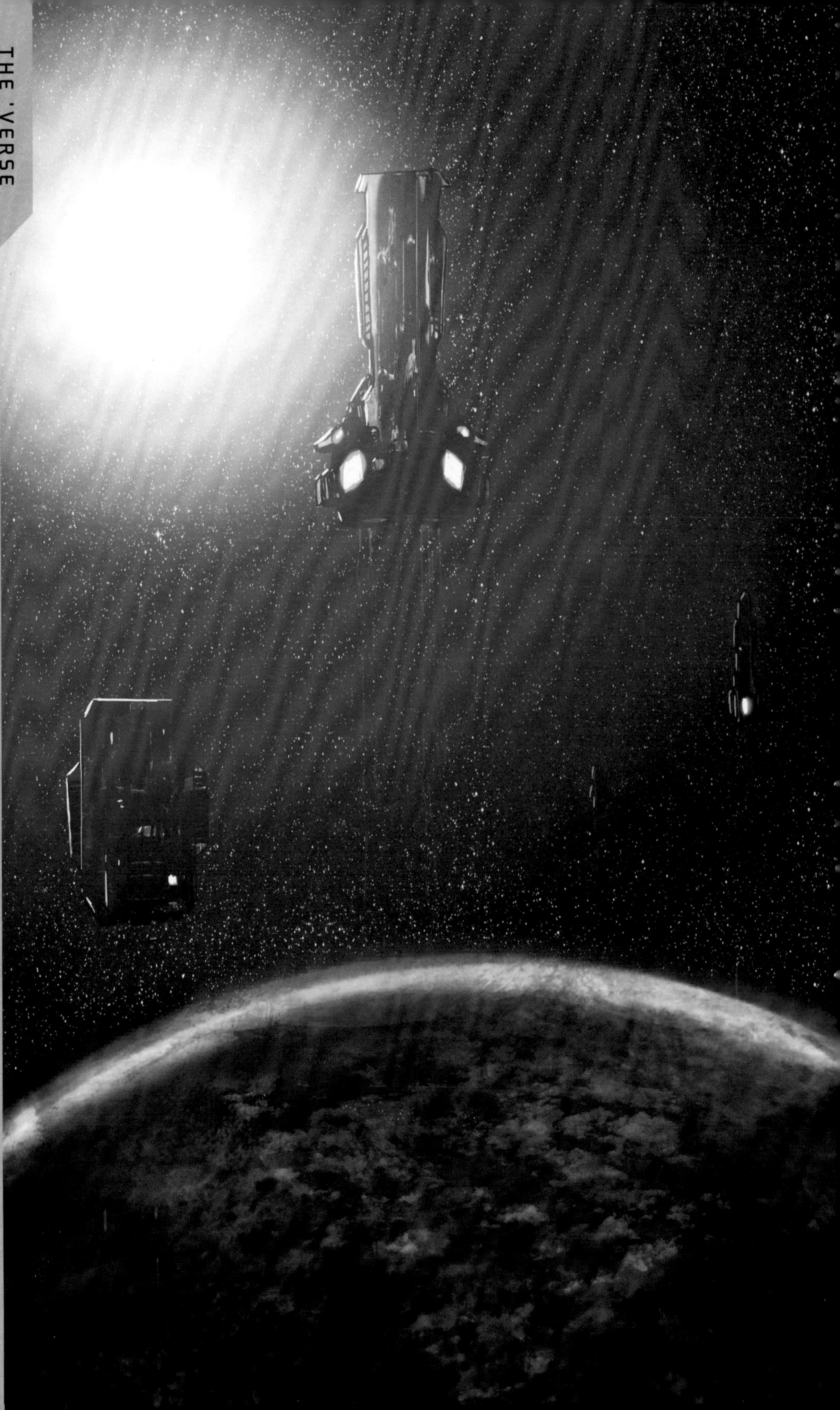

🏛 HISTORY

Despite the vastness of the 'Verse, all of its inhabitants actually originated on a single planet forty light-years from here. That planet, named Earth, was the cradle of human civilization and the beginning of our people's great journey across the stars.

For centuries, the people of Earth remained isolated on their planet, without the means for long-distance interstellar voyages. Their crude technology only allowed limited travel to nearby planets, often by unmanned craft. Despite being stuck on the ground, Earth's brightest minds kept their eyes on the stars.

In the year 2020, astronomers identified a cluster of stars, which they would designate 34 Tauri, that contained a number of planets that theoretically showed the proper conditions to sustain life. Though they did not yet have the means to reach these worlds, humanity would soon develop a great need to do so.

In the mid-twenty-first century, the damage that had been done to Earth by centuries of pollution and population growth reached the point where it could no longer be undone. The Earth had fewer than one hundred years before it would no longer be able to sustain human life. Thus, a plan had to be forged if the human race was to survive.

Working together, the nations of Earth formed an alliance and began to construct vast ships, known as Arks, to carry the population into the stars. Simultaneously, they developed technology capable of reshaping other worlds with unspoiled natural resources into habitable planets with the proper atmospheric and gravimetric conditions to allow humanity to thrive.

"Thrive" might be a bit of an exaggeration. —Zoë

While the people of Earth prepared to abandon their dying home, they sent this terraforming technology ahead of them to prepare their new worlds for habitation. Terraforming of planets in Earth's own solar system failed, so Earth turned its attention to the planets in the 34 Tauri cluster. The journey to those worlds would be a long one, taking over 120 years. Not a single inhabitant of Earth would live to call the 'Verse home, but their determination to survive would help chart the course for generations to come.

Over the last two hundred years since settlers initially arrived in the 'Verse, terraforming has been applied to nearly every planetary body in the system, offering the opportunity for settlers to claim their own place among the stars while still serving the greater good of the Alliance.

I always tend to forget about that last part... —Mal

Earth-That-Was may be nothing more than ancient history now, but with humanity no longer bound to one world, the possibilities are almost as endless as the universe itself.

THE CORE

When someone refers to the Core, they are referencing the Central Planets that revolve around the 'Verse's largest star, the White Sun (or Bai Hu). The Central Planets were some of the easiest to terraform and some of the earliest settled. They are viewed as the hub of civilization.

A view held primarily by those who have never bothered to venture beyond. —Book

 ## THE BORDER

Beyond the last of the Central Planets, on the other side of the Halo asteroid belt, two stars share an orbit around the White Sun. Any planets that circle these two stars, the Red Sun (Zhu Que) and Georgia (Huang Long), are referred to as Border Planets. Because these planets are further removed from the Core worlds, they tend to be a bit less regulated.

And a lot less civilized. —Simon

 ## THE RIM

Far beyond the Border, two more stars circle the White Sun—Kalidasa (Xuan Wu) and the Blue Sun (Qing Long). Because they are so far beyond the Core and Border, the worlds in the Rim have developed with little influence from outside forces.

That's what they want you to believe. —River

GETTING AROUND

The 'Verse is very large, and it is easy to become lost there. Small personal spacecraft are sufficient to make jumps between planets in the same system (or to a nearby moon), but they don't hold the fuel or supplies needed for longer journeys. And while large transports and luxury liners may seem better equipped for Core-to-Rim excursions, the cost of running them over such long distances has led to a drastic decrease in travel routes.

Fortunately, there is a mid-range option for travelers looking to explore the 'Verse freely without the constant fear of running out of fuel or money. A class of ship known as the mid-bulk transport was designed to deliver a small crew, its passengers, and its cargo safely between long-distance destinations. Although they may not be terribly pretty, mid-bulk transports (like the Allied Spacecraft Corporation's Firefly series) are the perfect answer for someone eager to explore the 'Verse.

You watch yourself, now. Serenity is perfectly lovely. —Kaylee

TERRAFORMING & HELIOFORMING

Terraforming is a process in which uninhabited planets are restructured to allow the possibility of human life. Terraforming uses advanced robotic equipment to dramatically alter a celestial body's ecological systems and physical traits, including composition of the atmosphere, temperature, gravitational pull, and availability of water.

The terraforming process can take decades to complete and can fail if a world lacks the required resources to fuel the process. The best results are found in worlds that are already close to habitable, like those found in the Core. These Earth-like planets only require subtle "tweaking" in their systems to allow human habitation.

Due to the needs of an ever-expanding population, all remaining planets and moons in the 'Verse have now been officially scheduled for terraforming.

Similar in concept to terraforming, *helioforming* is a process that condenses a brown dwarf and ignites it to create a miniature star known as a protostar. These artificially created stars offer additional warmth and light to terraformed planets that are a bit too far from their system's central star. There are seven of these man-made protostars located throughout the 'Verse.

 ## Did You Know?

· On Earth-That-Was, two nations led the charge when it came to the planet's mass evacuation—the United States of America and China. Their unique influences can still be found throughout much of the 'Verse's modern culture.

· Each of the five main stars in the 'Verse has two formal names, one Anglo (English) and one Sino (Chinese).

· A world on which terraforming has failed and is not capable of sustaining life is referred to as a "blackrock."

THE WHITE SUN SYSTEM (BAI HU)

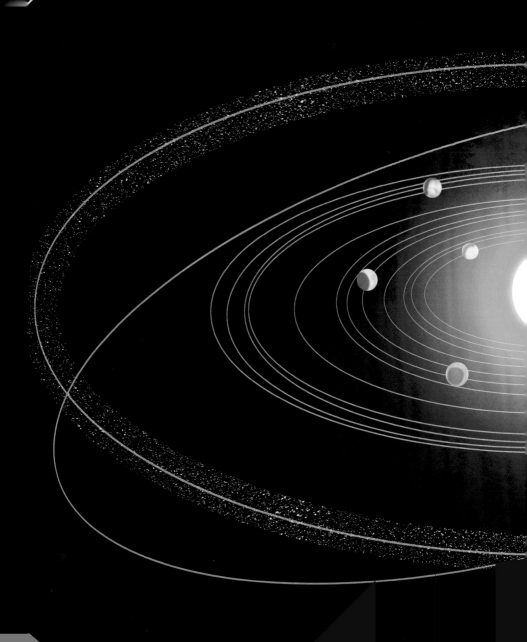

The White Sun is the central star around which the entirety of the 'Verse revolves. It makes sense, then, that the Central Planets orbiting closest to Bai Hu are considered some of the most important and influential worlds throughout all of human civilization. Guess when you pay for the book, you come out lookin' all shiny. —Mal

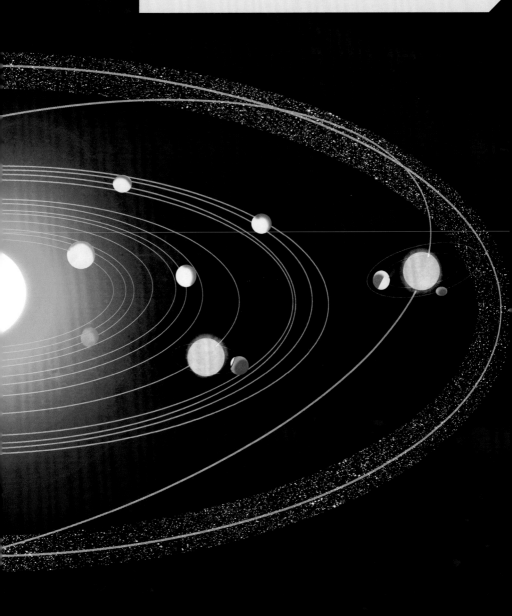

 ## HISTORY AND CULTURE

The White Sun system was initially selected for settlement due to the fact that many of its planets shared similarities with Earth-That-Was. However, Bai Hu itself is quite different from Sol, the star around which our planet of origin orbited. The White Sun's radius is two and a half times larger than Sol's, and it generates eighty times the amount of light. Fortunately, the planets that revolve around Bai Hu are a safe distance away from the star, residing in what scientists consider a "habitable zone."

The planets in the White Sun system were some of the earliest to be terraformed, thanks to their aforementioned similarities with Earth. Once settled, these planets began to flourish with the help of the Alliance—the governing body that presides over all planets in the 'Verse.

Rapid technological and medical advancements gave citizens of these Core planets the means to elevate their new civilization toward a brighter future. At the same time, the deep cultural history that was brought to these worlds by their original settlers allowed them to respect the ancient traditions of the past. This juxtaposition of new and old truly makes the Core planets unique in all of the 'Verse.

Clearly they ain't never seen River and Book together. Now that's a unique juxtaposition of new and old. —Zoë

Those who visit Core planets will find themselves surrounded by opportunity. These worlds are home to the 'Verse's most respected educational institutions and most affluent citizens. Food, shelter, and work are all readily available, and crime and disease are barely factors. The Alliance keeps a watchful eye on these planets to make sure that their peace and prosperity are properly maintained.

Londinium and Sihnon were the first planets to be settled and remain two of the most influential worlds in the White Sun system, yet a number of the other Core planets have made a name for themselves thanks to their contributions to the Alliance and the 'Verse as a whole. From the palatial estates of Bellerophon to the bioluminescent pools of Ariel, there is something for every traveler in the White Sun system. Once you've visited, you may never feel the urge to cross into the Border again.

MORE THAN A COUPLE HOURS IN THE CORE AND I'M ITCHIN' TO GET OUT. —JAYNE

I'm almost certain the feeling is mutual. —Inara

TIPS FOR A FUN TRIP

DO: Follow the rules. Alliance military presence is heaviest on the Core planets of the White Sun system, so you'll want to be on your best behavior. If you are a traveler who tends to like to take risks and stray beyond accepted boundaries, these are not the planets for you.

You heard 'em, Captain! ~Kaylee

DON'T: Stand out too much. The lower the profile you keep on a Core planet, the more likely you are to enjoy your visit. If you draw too much attention to yourself, even in ways that are not considered criminal, you may still find yourself paying an unplanned visit to an Alliance outpost for questioning.

Wouldn't be the first time. —Wash

DID YOU KNOW?

· The name "Bai Hu" means "white tiger," an ancient Chinese symbol representing the west, autumn, and metal.

· Two protostars, Qin Shi Huang and Lux, are helioformed brown dwarfs that orbit Bai Hu. They provide extra light and heat to the planets that orbit them.

· The Core planets of the White Sun system are surrounded by an asteroid belt called the Halo that separates them from Border worlds.

BERNADETTE

Bernadette was the first planet in the White Sun system, but it was not the first to be colonized. As mentioned, that honor falls to its neighboring worlds, Londinium and Sihnon. However, Bernadette has played a prominent role in the development of the 'Verse, serving as a staging ground for the Alliance's expansion operations for worlds located on the Border and in the Rim.

 ## HISTORY AND CULTURE

Londinium and Sihnon developed extremely different cultures from one another, due to the decidedly different heritages of their original settlers. As those planets became overcrowded in their earliest days, though, many of their citizens decided to take their chances on another newly terraformed world nearby. Bernadette became a melting pot planet, offering a unique blend of traditions and religions from Earth-That-Was, both Eastern and Western in origin. In many ways, Bernadette's cultural combinations served as a model for other new worlds as settlers began to spread across the 'Verse.

 ## SIGHTS AND ACTIVITIES

Alliance Colony and Settlement Authority: Although its proximity to the White Sun makes Bernadette the closest planet to the center of the 'Verse, it has become an essential stop for any settler looking to stake a claim on any outer world, as it is home to the Alliance Colony and Settlement Authority. If a little ranch on a moon in the Georgia system is calling your name, it's best to swing by Bernadette first to make sure the purchase is legal and sanctioned by the Alliance.

OR, you could just rush in, guns a-blazin', and take it for yourself. You know, like normal folks do. —JAYNE

LONDINIUM

Londinium is perhaps the planet that most closely resembles Earth-That-Was, so it's no wonder that it became home to one of the earliest settlements in the 'Verse. Since then, Londinium has evolved into one of the most prominent Core worlds and serves as the seat of government of the Union of Allied Planets.

HISTORY AND CULTURE

The second planet in the White Sun system, Londinium was one of the first in the 'Verse to be terraformed and populated (along with its sister planet Sihnon). The majority of Londinium's citizens are directly descended from settlers whose origins trace back to the Western civilizations on Earth-That-Was.

Londinium is home to the Alliance Parliament, the body that oversees the rule of law in the 'Verse. While each planet and moon in the 'Verse has its own governing officials and local laws, the Parliament administers the crucial policies that span from the White Sun all the way to the Blue Sun. With the 'Verse's governing body housed on the planet, it is only natural that Londinium would also have a heightened military presence to protect elected officials from those renegades foolish enough to rebel against Alliance rule.

Now who would go and do such a thing? —Mal

Much of the architecture on Londinium harkens back to the classic gothic architecture of Earth-That-Was, combining current technological advancements with ancient design techniques to create a stunning blend of classic and modern. This veneration for human history is also reflected in many of the cultural institutions found on Londinium that celebrate the 'Verse and its origins.

ETIQUETTE

Londinium is a frequent destination for visiting dignitaries and influential figures from throughout the system, making it one of the most formal planets in the 'Verse. If you're visiting Londinium from a Border world, be sure to brush up on your manners first. *Been practicin' my curtsy. —Kaylee*

GETTING AROUND

There are twenty-six major metropolises on Londinium, including the capital city of New Cardiff, all connected by mass transit. Londinium is also home to five impressive spaceports that offer regular transport to destinations both on planet and off. The ports can get quite crowded during peak seasons, so be sure to confirm your travel plans before arrival.

SIGHTS AND ACTIVITIES

Londinium Museum: The fabled Londinium Museum is a repository of important artifacts, some of which are older than the 'Verse itself. The museum is divided into two sections, one focusing on human history and the other on classic art. While most of the items on display date back to Londinium's earliest settlers, some priceless artifacts have even survived from Earth-That-Was.

There's quite a secondary market for antiques like these. —Zoë

DON'T bother with ANY PRICELESS ONES, though. ONly stEAl the ONES worth somethin'. —JAYNE

SIHNON

Another of the most significant Core Planets in the 'Verse, Sihnon is the third world to circle the White Sun. With approximately 5.3 billion inhabitants, Sihnon may seem overly crowded upon first visit, but it quickly becomes evident that its citizens have achieved a level of sophistication and technological advancement unimaginable on most Border worlds.

🏛 HISTORY AND CULTURE

Sihnon was one of the very first Core Planets to be terraformed by the Alliance's robotic crews, circa 2220, in advance of settlers arriving in the White Sun system. The process took years to complete but eventually created a world that many travelers have since dubbed the most beautiful in the 'Verse.

Sihnon is covered with glorious mountains, peaceful valleys, gentle rivers, and bubbling hot springs that make dusty Border worlds seem like desolate wastelands in comparison. The planet is easily recognizable from space due to its reddish hue, but as you enter atmo, you are bound to be dazzled by the gleaming capital city, Lu'Weng, which has been described by many travelers as "an ocean of light." This incandescent beauty sets the tone for the wide array of dazzling wonders found on Sihnon's surface.

If her home planet's so dang pretty, what's Inara doin' out here with us? —Mal

I ask myself that every day. —Inara

Sihnon's orbit lies just beyond that of Londinium, but despite their general proximity and equal prominence within the Bai Hu system, the two planets' cultures and origins could not be more different. Whereas Londinium was primarily settled by those who descended from the Western cultures of Earth-That-Was,

Sihnon's settlers were mainly of Eastern origin. Though seemingly a minor disparity, the planets evolved on completely unique cultural paths due to these simple differences in tradition.

Most citizens of Sihnon primarily speak Mandarin and practice Buddhism. In fact, Sihnon has become the destination of choice for those studying this ancient religion due to its high concentration of temples and monasteries. Many of these temples house important religious artifacts and tomes dating back to the earliest days of Earth-That-Was.

Sounds like your kinda place, Shepherd. —Kaylee

Slightly different beliefs, but I try to keep an open mind. —Book

Sihnon is also the home of the 'Verse's trade associations, including the Companion's Guild—a union of professional courtesans respected across the 'Verse for their grace, skill, and beauty. Though the Guild's network of training houses has since spread to many other planets, the best Companions are still said to have honed their craft at Sihnon's oldest and most traditional houses, such as the legendary House Madrassa.

Bet I could teach those gals a few things! —JAYNE

You wouldn't last five minutes with a certified Companion. —Inara

That's about four more minutes than he'd need... —Wash

🛍 SHOPPING AND ENTERTAINMENT

Sihnon is well known for its luxurious garments, spun from pure silk harvested across the planet. Lu'Weng is not just the capital of Sihnon but also the capital of its fashion industry. Here, artisans use time-tested techniques to weave beautiful scarves, dresses, and kimonos that are as high in quality as they are in price. Styles effortlessly combine ageless tradition with futuristic flare, making "old-fashioned" the most talked about new fashion. Sihnon's latest trends are always the hottest—and most counterfeited—in the 'Verse.

You can get a cheap knockoff at any port for about a third of the price. —Kaylee

GETTING AROUND

In order to preserve both the planet's culture and its resources, Sihnon's government has restricted travel to and from the planet by large vessels. This makes visiting Sihnon a bit more challenging for travelers without their own personal craft. The government does allow for limited travel into nonequatorial areas, but even that is heavily regulated and often requires express written permission from the authorities. It is best to plan your trips to Sihnon far in advance so that you can apply for the proper access permits in a timely manner.

Or just sneak in when they ain't lookin'. —Zoë

TIPS FOR A FUN TRIP

DO: Schedule a tour of a Companion house while in Sihnon. Even if pleasure is not on your agenda, the Guild's ancient traditions and exquisite taste in decor can be appreciated by even the most conservative of travelers.

Why wouldn't PLEASURE be on your agenda?! —JAYNE

DON'T: Expect free samples. Companions are highly skilled in all aspects of their craft—which includes self-defense. House tours are strictly on a "look, but don't touch" basis.

What a shame. —Wash

Oh, is that so? —Zoë

Only for men who aren't blissfully wed, of course, lambie toes! —Wash

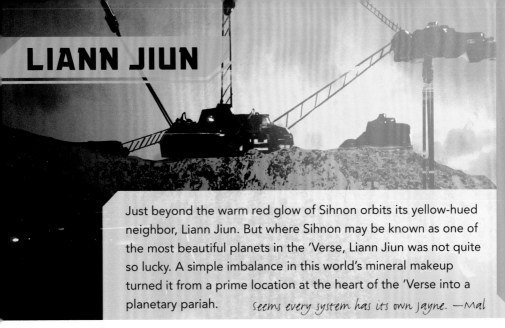

LIANN JIUN

Just beyond the warm red glow of Sihnon orbits its yellow-hued neighbor, Liann Jiun. But where Sihnon may be known as one of the most beautiful planets in the 'Verse, Liann Jiun was not quite so lucky. A simple imbalance in this world's mineral makeup turned it from a prime location at the heart of the 'Verse into a planetary pariah. *seems every system has its own Jayne. —Mal*

 ## HISTORY AND CULTURE

An overabundance of sulfur generated as a byproduct of terraforming Liann Jiun provided the planet its signature color, as well as a pungent smell that kept away many of the upper class citizens that would normally populate a Core world. This opened the planet to settlers who were desperate for land but unable to pay the premium prices found on other Core planets with slightly more pleasant odors.

After a few months on this boat, I imagine even Liann Jiun smells like roses. —Inara

Because of the sulfur's key role in the production of gunpowder, Liann Jiun also become home to the Alliance Navy's munitions factories. These facilities, as well as the sulfur mines, are the primary source of employment for the planet's working-class settlers.

 ## LODGING

Squalid Springs Spa: Many travelers make the mistake of bypassing Liann Jiun due to its atmo's rancid reputation. However, the planet has many natural wonders that cannot be found on other Core worlds, including hot sulfur springs that are said to have amazing healing effects. One luxury resort, the Squalid Springs Spa, offers a wide variety of wellness packages that are guaranteed to help guests forget about their noses and focus on the rest of their bodies.

Because nothing relaxes me like the aroma of rotten eggs. —Wash

GONGHE

Most travelers in the 'Verse are used to seeing herds of cows and sheep on Border Planets, but few terraformed worlds were ever populated with many species beyond essential livestock. For a large number of settlers, the ancient animals of Earth-That-Was are now nothing more than fairy tales. But there's one planet where many of those forgotten species still thrive—Gonghe, the fifth planet in the White Sun system.

HISTORY AND CULTURE

Humans weren't the only species brought to the 'Verse from Earth-That-Was. In fact, thousands of species of animals and insects were transported on the Arks, arriving at their new home on the sanctuary planet of Gonghe. Its wide variety of natural ecosystems and its pristine air and water made Gonghe the perfect location to preserve some of the rarest creatures in all of creation. With conservation and breeding programs overseen by Alliance scientists and heightened security to prevent illegal poaching activities, Gonghe is a wildlife refuge unlike anything else in the 'Verse.

We tried to borrow a hippo once. It did not end well. —Zoë

 # SIGHTS AND ACTIVITIES

White Sun Zoo: Although Gonghe is not open to settlers for habitation, a small area of the planet does welcome visitors who would like to learn more about the species that live here. The White Sun Zoo spans hundreds of acres, simulating the natural habitats found across the planet to showcase some of the unusual creatures that dwell there—from penguins and platypuses to tigers and termites. Gonghe's highly knowledgeable scientific support crew offers safari tours of the regions beyond the zoo grounds for a premium price. All proceeds benefit the Alliance's conservation efforts.

Think they'd let us trade Jayne in for something slightly more intelligent? —Wash

RUBICON

Rubicon is one of the few Core worlds still undergoing the terraforming process. This planet was bypassed for centuries due to an inherent lack of natural resources that made it the least suited Core planet for colonization. While it was originally far more effective to generate livable worlds further out on the Border, recent advancements in terraforming technology—coupled with rising overpopulation rates on many Core worlds—inspired the Alliance to give Rubicon another chance.

With the terraforming process nearing completion, the planet is expected to be open for colonization by late 2519.

And by 2520, there'll likely be more trendy juice bars than settlers. —Mal

[?] DID YOU KNOW?

· Rubicon is the only planet in the White Sun system that does not have any moons orbiting it.

· Before terraforming, Rubicon was frequently used as a docking station for many of the Alliance Navy's largest cruisers when traveling through the Core.

· Openings frequently become available on Rubicon's terraforming crew. No prior experience necessary.

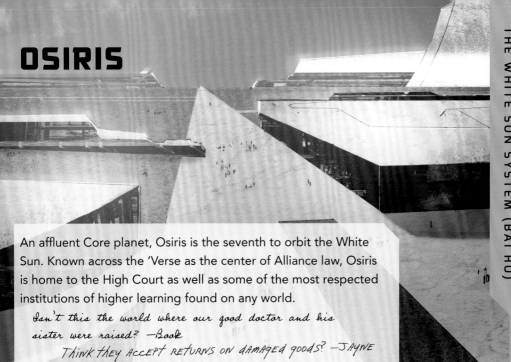

OSIRIS

An affluent Core planet, Osiris is the seventh to orbit the White Sun. Known across the 'Verse as the center of Alliance law, Osiris is home to the High Court as well as some of the most respected institutions of higher learning found on any world.

Isn't this the world where our good doctor and his sister were raised? —Book

THINK THEY ACCEPT RETURNS ON DAMAGED GOODS? —JAYNE

 ## HISTORY AND CULTURE

Londinium and Sihnon may be viewed as the two most significant planets in the 'Verse, but many would argue that Osiris comes in a close third. Whereas Londinium is home to the system's government and Sihnon is the center of trade and culture, Osiris is where justice is served in the 'Verse.

Captain, chart a course for anywhere but here. —Zoë

Not only is Capital City the location of the High Court that presides over the entire system, but it is also the place to be for young students eager to study and practice the law. The University of Osiris is considered the most prestigious law school in all of the 'Verse.

Learning the complex laws of the Alliance is no simple task, but breaking those laws on Osiris can be far easier than anticipated. The planet is constantly monitored by a network of surveillance equipment designed to keep its citizens safe. That hasn't stopped an unsavory criminal network from developing on the planet though, so always be sure to stick to popular tourist areas and steer clear of unfamiliar territory.

 ## GETTING AROUND

Traversing Osiris is easy, thanks to a vast mass transit system and pedestrian-friendly cities. But as easy as it is to get where you need to be, there are still some areas you need to avoid. The planet has a number of "blackout zones," areas where the Alliance's surveillance network is nonfunctional. These zones are

illegal to enter under any circumstances, so make sure to pay attention to any posted warnings. If you wander into one, even if you just made a wrong turn, you will be arrested and prosecuted without question. *They aren't kidding. Trust me. —Simon*

 ## DINING AND NIGHTLIFE

Underworld: A popular club near the campus of the University of Osiris, this student hotspot takes inspiration from the planet's namesake, Osiris, the Egyptian god of the dead. Decked out in desert decor, this watering hole may not be the perfect oasis, but it's a great place for the planet's younger set to unwind and escape the pressure of their parents' high expectations for a night. As long as you don't mind a few intoxicated undergrads, you're in for a legendary time.

 ## TIPS FOR A FUN TRIP

DO: Visit the statue of Hippocrates. Located near the University's fabled MedAcad, this impressive marble statue is a solemn reminder of the oath that young doctors-in-training swear to upon graduation.

DON'T: Visit the statue near graduation day. It's a strange tradition for Osiris's fresh crop of surgeons to climb on top of the sculpture in various states of undress (and sobriety) and sing the University's alma mater at the top of their lungs.

Thought Simon said it was the national anthem. —Kaylee

My recollection may be a bit foggy.... —Simon

SANTO

Santo is the lone planet orbiting the White Sun system's first protostar, Qin Shi Huang. Although Santo is considered one of the Core worlds due to its location, its culture more closely resembles something one would find far out on the Border.

 ## HISTORY AND CULTURE

As Core worlds go, Santo is one of the youngest . . . and it shows. Because its protostar, Qin Shi Huang, was the last in the 'Verse to be helioformed, Santo trailed behind its neighboring planets when it came to colonization. Sadly, it never quite caught up.

These days, Santo tends to be used primarily as a pit stop for crews who need to refuel and unwind during the long trips between other Core planets. The world's populace proudly describes themselves as "rough around the edges," a factor that doesn't necessarily add to Santo's appeal for the average traveler. Even the Alliance has limited its presence on this world. For those very reasons, Santo has become a haven for slavers and other criminals looking to keep a low profile after their latest score.

Which makes it our kinda place. —Jayne

ETIQUETTE

None. Santo is a backward planet that may seem a bit out of place when compared to its neighboring planets in the Core. When visiting Santo, an enlightening conversation may not be easy to find, but as long as you can spit and curse, you'll fit right in.

Perhaps it would be best if I stay on the ship. — Simon

DINING AND NIGHTLIFE

Only Chance Saloon: Whether you're looking for a stiff drink or to win a few bucks playing pool, this rundown bar is the best that Santo has to offer, which isn't saying much. Bring a few extra credits, as management takes no responsibility for frequent failure of the billiard balls on the holo-table. And always be prepared for a fight. The clientele here is notoriously dangerous, so there's a good chance you'll be chasing your whiskey with a swift punch to the jaw.

Exactly how I like it. — Mal   *I will be sure to remember that. — Inara*

DID YOU KNOW?

· The name "Santo" translates to "Saint" from a number of languages, an odd choice for a planet that clearly has none of those living on it.

· The planet has many temperate regions that are quite lovely, despite their general lack of culture. Santo's inhabitants have tried on multiple occasions to develop their world into a resort destination for wealthy travelers, but the efforts have never succeeded.

· Slavers make frequent stops on Santo after delivering their "goods," and they are always looking to refresh their precious human cargo. Be cautious or you might find yourself involuntarily recruited on to a terraforming crew bound for a distant moon.

See, Doc? Told you it could be worse. — Mal

Yes . . . River and I are forever grateful to be one small step above forced servitude. — Simon

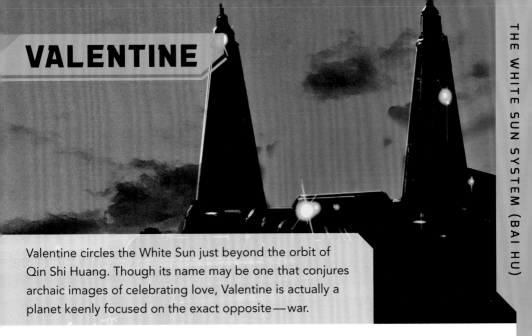

VALENTINE

Valentine circles the White Sun just beyond the orbit of Qin Shi Huang. Though its name may be one that conjures archaic images of celebrating love, Valentine is actually a planet keenly focused on the exact opposite — war.

HISTORY AND CULTURE

Valentine is the home base of the Union of Allied Planets Navy, making it the centerpiece of the 'Verse's impressive military complex. This highly developed world serves as the central command center for all Alliance tactical operations, and all of the inhabitants on this world are required to have maximum-security clearance. Visitors are not welcome unless they are planning to enlist.

WHAT TO WEAR

If you're visiting Valentine, you're likely a high-ranking Alliance official, so be sure to have your uniform carefully pressed and your medals on straight.

Only own one coat. Have a feeling the color wouldn't go over well here. —Mal

GETTING AROUND

Entry into Valentine's airspace is strictly prohibited to ships without proper authorization, and unidentified craft will be shot down. Military escorts accompany even those ships that have been granted permission to enter atmo, accompanying them to their designated docking location.

Suddenly, Valentine's Day doesn't sound nearly as sweet. —Zoë

LODGING

While there are no hotels on Valentine, there are a generous number of barracks available for officers returning from long patrols and for visiting dignitaries from throughout the 'Verse. There are also plenty of secure cells available for any uninvited guests that manage to make their way to the planet's surface.

Does that mean you'll forgive me for not getting you a gift? —Wash

Not a chance, dear. —Zoë

33

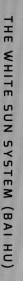

BELLEROPHON

Bellerophon is home to some of the richest people in the 'Verse, who live in exclusive floating estates high above the planet's largest sea. Few can afford to live on this world, but a quick visit to experience Bellerophon's opulence firsthand is certainly worth the price.

 ## HISTORY AND CULTURE

When wealthy landowners, businessmen, and Alliance officers find the need to escape the rapid pace of the 'Verse, Bellerophon is where they go. This world is the ultimate escape from everyday life, offering a perfect mix of indulgence and discretion. With amenities regularly shipped in from other planets and automated services to take care of your needs, you'll never have to lift a finger during your stay.

We'll be glad to lift it for you... along with any other valuables you might have. —Mal

ETIQUETTE

If you have the money to live on Bellerophon, you can likely act however you want. If you do something wrong, it's almost certain that you have enough credits to buy your way out of trouble.

If you happen to be visiting Bellerophon or work for one of the many off-world companies that supply the planet's citizens, however, be sure that you have all of your documents in order and that you do not overstep your bounds. The wealthier your host, the higher their security and the lower their tolerance.

 ## GETTING AROUND

As the vast majority of the planet's population resides a mile above the open water, a small ship is required. Good maneuverability is a must, as the winds from the Bellerophon Sea below can often make it difficult to hold a ship steady during docking.

*Or when trying to steal garbage.
(It's a long story.) —Wash*

 ## LODGING

Bellerophon Estates: Who needs to live on land when you can hover above the Bellerophon Sea in your own private palace? Each estate is the size of a small town, offering only the finest in luxury living to its tenants. Some of these estates have been converted into high-end resorts for travelers willing to pay top dollar for comfort and privacy. *while others are owned by rich, lonely folks just waitin' to get fleeced. —Zoë*

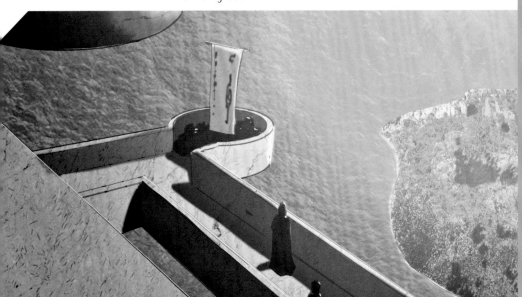

DINING AND NIGHTLIFE

Since Bellerophon is a hotbed of high society, there are frequent galas and fundraisers thrown at the planet's private residences. If you can find a way into one, you may be fortunate enough to see exquisite collections of art and artifacts that date back to Earth-That-Was.

SIGHTS AND ACTIVITIES

Isis Canyon: Few visitors to Bellerophon ever bother to leave the comfort of their estates. For those who prefer to keep their feet firmly on dry land, however, there's no patch of land drier than Isis Canyon. Though this stretch of desert may seem barren and lonely to most, it has a natural beauty to it that you just can't find locked in a gilded cage floating above the sea.

I do believe clothing is optional, isn't that right, Captain? —Inara

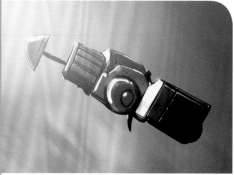

TIPS FOR A FUN TRIP

DO: Get an invitation. Security can be unusually high on Bellerophon, thanks to the status of the planet's denizens. Regular Alliance patrols are heightened here compared to most planets, and some residents even hire personal security services to defend their large collections of valuables. Unwanted guests are certain to be shown just how unwelcome they are.

DON'T: Take home a souvenir. Many of the Bellerophon Estates are equipped with high-end antitheft systems that alert an occupant when an item of high value is being moved or removed without permission. As tempting as it might be to put that expensive trinket in your suitcase, someone will almost certainly notice.

Challenge accepted. —Mal

ARIEL

The eleventh planet in the White Sun system, Ariel is the place to go when you need the best medical attention the 'Verse can offer. No appointments are necessary, however, to experience the wide range of high culture and natural beauty abundant on this world.

 ## HISTORY AND CULTURE

Ariel is all about balance. Although the planet is known for its technological developments, especially in the field of medicine, it is also respected for its devotion to the arts. Its gleaming cities are home to renowned hospitals as well as beautiful museums and some of the finest restaurants in the Core.

While Ariel may have dozens of interesting urban centers to explore, visitors prefer to step away from the city and enjoy the untouched splendor of its planetary park system. With activities from hiking to swimming, Ariel appeals to the nature lover who doesn't want to stray too far toward the Rim.

It's like folks in the Core ain't never seen a gorramn tree before. —Jayne

GETTING AROUND

The skies above Ariel's major cities are congested with personal craft, not to mention larger vessels regularly launching from the planet's four spaceports. It seems that the only surefire way to get around Ariel freely is in one of the many official medical vehicles serving its hospitals. Unfortunately, the chances of you riding in one of those transports are slim without sustaining a major injury.

Unless you can salvage one and rebuild it for yourself, that is . . . ~Kaylee

 ## WHAT TO WEAR

All respectable attire is welcome on the streets of Ariel. However, if you're not in scrubs or a white coat, you might feel out of place. *Fortunately, I remembered to pack mine. — Simon*

IN CASE OF EMERGENCY

St. Lucy's Medical Center: Located in Ariel City, St. Lucy's is perhaps the most sophisticated hospital in the 'Verse. Whether you have been mortally wounded by a band of Browncoat brigands or are merely required by Companion's Guild law to submit to an annual checkup, the esteemed medical professionals in this facility will be sure to fix whatever ails you with skill and grace.

They almost make all the pokin' and proddin' sound tolerable. —Zoë

It never is. —Inara

SIGHTS AND ACTIVITIES

Bioluminescent Lake: One of the wonders of Ariel's vast park system is a lake that emits a brilliant glow, thanks to the chemical reactions of microorganisms that dwell within it. Vacationers come from across the 'Verse to swim in its cool waters as they light up the night.

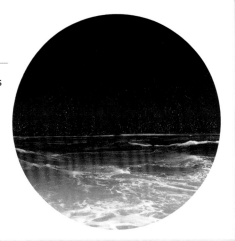

TIPS FOR A FUN TRIP

DO: Bring proper ID. While most Core planets have a strong Alliance presence, that is especially true on Ariel due to the sensitive nature of the medical profession. Pharmaceuticals are often the target of criminal endeavors, so expect to be scanned a bit more frequently during your visits.

Nurse Beauma Sclevages, reporting for duty! —Wash

DON'T: Fake your ID. Although forgeries are readily available through back channels, there's one door on Ariel that you'll quickly discover a false IdentCard can't open—the one to your prison cell! Unless you're a certified medical professional, turn the other way.

We applied the cortical electrodes, but were unable to get a neural reaction from either patient. —Jayne

ALBION

The 'Verse was built upon centuries of significant scientific breakthroughs that allowed mankind to traverse the stars and create new worlds on which to dwell. The proud scientific tradition of the Alliance continues in the White Sun system on the planet Albion.

🏛 HISTORY AND CULTURE

If you want to serve as a doctor, you go to Ariel. If you want to practice the law, you go to Osiris. But if you want to help create the cutting edge technology that helps to make the 'Verse a better place, then Albion is the destination for you. This planet-sized think tank is a haven for scientists and engineers looking to push the boundaries of modern technology to help revolutionize life on every world from the Core to the Rim. Researchers on Albion have created everything from revolutionary medicines and water purification systems to faster starship engines and improved terraforming equipment.

But have they invented a compression coil that won't bust? I didn't think so! —Kaylee

❓ DID YOU KNOW?

· While countless 'Verse-changing innovations have been developed on Albion, products are not actually mass-produced here. Once approved by the Alliance, manufacturing of these items takes place on industrial worlds further toward the Rim, like Beaumonde.

Let 'em have their shiny toys. We got everythin' we need right here. —Mal

Except money. —Zoë

And Ammo. —Jayne

· Experiments that may prove dangerous, such as those involving powerful weaponry or toxic chemical agents, are conducted on Albion's R&D moon, Avalon.

And jobs. —Wash

And real food. —Simon

· Research on Albion and Avalon are funded by the Alliance, allowing government agencies early access and implementation of any newtech developed there.

And a ship if you don't all bì zuĭ! —Mal

PERSEPHONE

Tucked away at the outer edge of the White Sun system, orbiting the protostar Lux, sits Persephone. This world serves as the gateway between the Core and the Border, not only because of its location, but also because of its unique blend of cultures and traditions that span the 'Verse.

 ## HISTORY AND CULTURE

Persephone is unique among the Central Planets thanks to its placement near the furthest edge of the system. Because it is one of the first stops in (and out) of the Core, the planet naturally developed into the perfect port world. With six major ports and an Alliance transport hub, Persephone is an essential stop for any crew's journey to the Border and beyond.

Docking on Persephone is made easy thanks to regulations set in place by the Alliance and the Trader's Guild, who oversees the inspection and taxation of

all cargo entering and leaving the system. And once you're planetside, you'll find a strange cultural dichotomy that accurately represents how different the Core and Border can be.

Port areas, like the Eavesdown Docks, are bustling with people from all over the 'Verse. Vendors sell their wares, refugees bribe their way onto ships, and mechanics scavenge for crucial parts. This is where good honest captains look for their next job, while seasoned criminals look for their next mark. Commerce is heavily monitored at these ports, yet the culture feels strangely unrestricted . . . and often a bit dangerous.   *Always knew there was a reason we fit in here so well. —Zoë*

The planet's major cities, however, are far more sophisticated, in line with what you would find on most Core planets. The cultural divide between the planet's most wealthy citizens and its lower class has also resulted in a higher crime rate in some areas, requiring a heightened Alliance presence in important cities like the planet's capital, Demeter.

Persephone offers the rare chance to experience the excitement of the Border and the refinement of the Core on a single world. You may have only planned to stop there to fuel up, but make sure you take the time to get out and explore!

ETIQUETTE

Because Persephone straddles the edges of the Core and Border, sometimes unusual situations can arise from the unexpected clash of cultures. What may seem like a common gesture to you may in fact be a great insult to a member of the planet's high society. Choose your words and actions carefully, as you never know when you might accidentally find yourself challenging someone to a duel!

That certainly would be unfortunate…—Inara

 ## GETTING AROUND

Since Persephone is a primarily a port planet, getting around is a relatively painless process. The docks are designed for frequent arrivals and departures of mid-bulk to large vessels, yet the streets surrounding those docks are best traversed on foot due to steady crowds of pedestrian traffic. Larger cities are more welcoming to personal craft and offer mass transit options, including an elevated train system.

Of course, if you're on Persephone, you may be more interested in how to travel off the planet than how to travel on it. Fortunately, passage on a transport ship can be easily arranged. In fact, many of the ships are so eager to make a few extra credits by adding paid passengers to their berths that they will set up outside their ship and actively court potential travelers. Occasionally, a bidding war can occur, with desperate crews offering prospective passengers increasingly better incentives to choose their ship for a journey.

Who are they callin' desperate?! ~Kaylee

 ## SIGHTS AND ACTIVITIES

Southdown Abbey: This secluded abbey is located on the outskirts of Persephone's capital city of Demeter. Although not nearly as impressive as some of the gothic religious structures found on Londinium and Sihnon, the kind Shepherds who dwell here will gladly invite you into their humble home to share both their teachings and a fresh meal grown in their lush gardens.

Some days I do miss that life. —Book
THEN YOU SEE MY SMILIN' FACE. —JAYNE
And I miss it even more. —Book

 ## SHOPPING AND ENTERTAINMENT

Eavesdown Docks: One of Persephone's largest spaceports, the Eavesdown Docks are a perfect place for weary crews to touch down as they travel between the Core and Border worlds. The docks are not only a great place to refuel and reload but also to find new jobs, new passengers, and even new crewmembers. If

you're not ready to think about your next mission, though, the Eavesdown Docks offer a wide variety of shops and vendor stalls, selling everything from bizarre street food to some of the most unusual—and occasionally questionable—fashion choices in the Core.

It's almost as if they're trying to pick a fight with our sweet little Kaylee. —Wash

DINING AND NIGHTLIFE

Grand Ball: If you're on Persephone at the right time of year and are fortunate enough to get your name on the carefully curated guest list, this prestigious cotillion attended by all of the most respected members of Persephone's high society is not to be missed. Elegant ladies in expensive gowns promenade beneath a floating chandelier as the movers and shakers of the planet's upper crust make deals and trade stories. Add an extravagant spread of food and

delightful music, and you have what most consider to be the social event of the season. Attendance is by invitation only. Proper dress is required and weapons are strictly forbidden.

Quite a shindig, if I recall. —Mal

How could we ever forget? —Inara

? DID YOU KNOW?

- Persephone was one of the three planets (along with Hera and Shadow) that played vital roles in the Unification War between the Independent rebellion and the Alliance.

- One of Persephone's two moons, Renao, is mostly covered in water. The few islands on the moon's surface are privately owned resorts.

- Although duels may seem like a fairly common way to defend one's honor in the 'Verse, don't bother loading your pistol on Persephone. Duels here are fought with swords instead!

Knew I should have read this book a touch sooner... —Mal

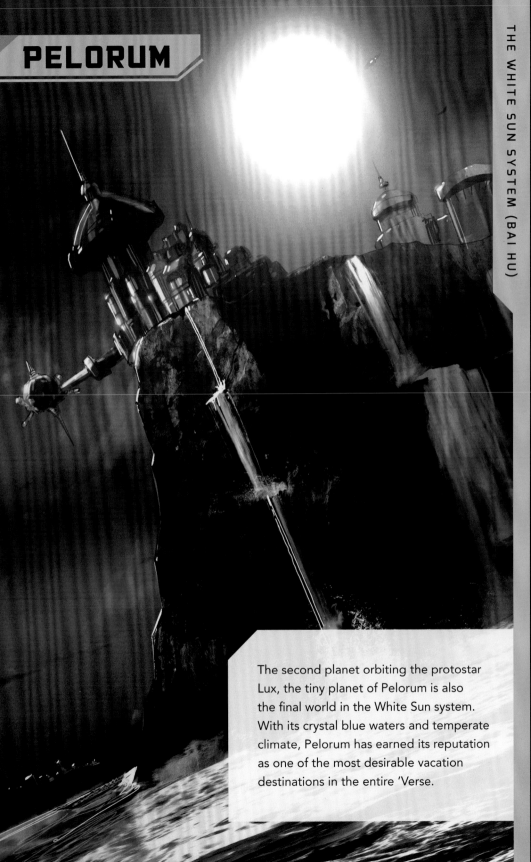

PELORUM

The second planet orbiting the protostar Lux, the tiny planet of Pelorum is also the final world in the White Sun system. With its crystal blue waters and temperate climate, Pelorum has earned its reputation as one of the most desirable vacation destinations in the entire 'Verse.

HISTORY AND CULTURE

The further you get toward the Border, the more likely you are to get a bit of sand in your boots. But if you prefer that sand to come from the beach rather than the desert, Pelorum is the planet for you. That is, if you can afford to stay there.

Most of the planet's surface is devoted to resorts so exclusive and expensive that they'll make you wonder if the name of Pelorum's host protostar is actually short for "Luxurious." While the steep prices tend to limit Pelorum's clientele to the wealthiest members of Core society, the planet often finds itself host to crews coming home from a big job—or a big heist—who are looking to unwind in style.

No matter where you're from, though, if you have the credits to spare, Pelorum is the perfect place to relax and recover from a long journey across the 'Verse.

I tend to find such indulgences unnecessary. —Book

No problem, padre. That just means more indulgences for us. —Jayne

LODGING

The Windfall: A majestic casino and hotel perched atop a cascading waterfall, the Windfall makes the other resorts on Pelorum look like backwater inns on the outskirts of the Rim. Single rooms at the Windfall can cost thousands of credits per night, but for high rollers who seek only the most opulent accommodations the amenities can't be beat—including unlimited food and beverages, concierge service, spa access, private pools and beaches, in-room Cortex feeds, and monogrammed bathrobes.

I ever get a bathrobe with my initials on it, I ain't never wearin' anythin' else ever again. —Zoë

Is that a promise, honey dumpling? —Wash

WHAT TO WEAR

Lux's rays can get pretty intense during the day, and they're only intensified when reflected off Pelorum's rippling oceans. Though you may not choose to wear much else here, at least put on a healthy coat of sunscreen. After all, you came to Pelorum to burn your money, not your skin.

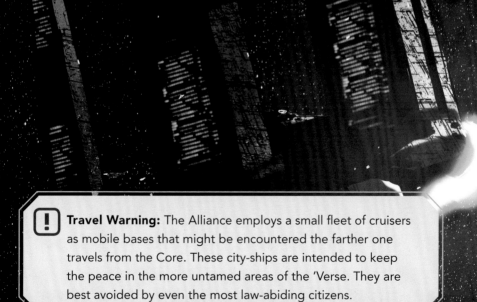

Travel Warning: The Alliance employs a small fleet of cruisers as mobile bases that might be encountered the farther one travels from the Core. These city-ships are intended to keep the peace in the more untamed areas of the 'Verse. They are best avoided by even the most law-abiding citizens.

THE GEORGIA SYSTEM (HUANG LONG)

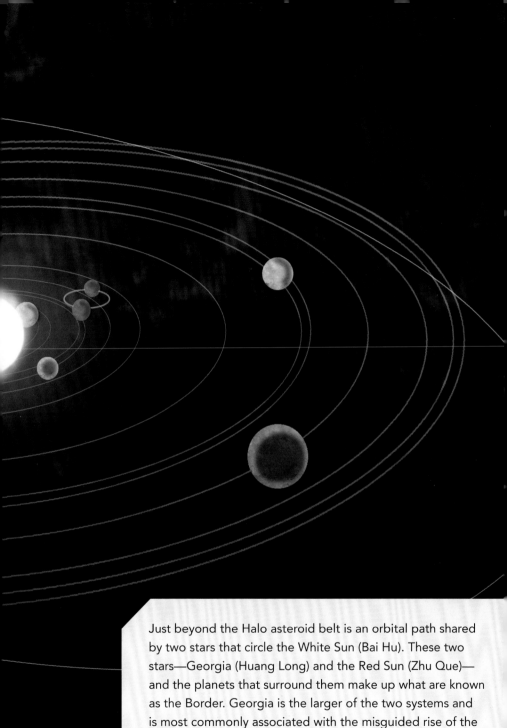

Just beyond the Halo asteroid belt is an orbital path shared by two stars that circle the White Sun (Bai Hu). These two stars—Georgia (Huang Long) and the Red Sun (Zhu Que)—and the planets that surround them make up what are known as the Border. Georgia is the larger of the two systems and is most commonly associated with the misguided rise of the Independent Planets.

Ain't nothin' "misguided" about freedom. —Mal

HISTORY AND CULTURE

Once the Core worlds surrounding Bai Hu were settled, some of the 'Verse's more adventurous citizens began looking beyond the White Sun system for a place that they could truly call their own. Fortunately, there were plenty of planets surrounding the other stars in the 'Verse just waiting to be terraformed and populated.

The settlers who came to Georgia weren't looking to re-create what had been built in the Core. In many cases, the fast-paced, government-approved lifestyle found on the Central Planets was exactly what they were trying to escape. Instead, the worlds surrounding Georgia were developed with simpler things in mind, focusing more on common tasks that would keep families fed and healthy while avoiding the excesses now found in the big cities on Londinium, Sihnon, and so many other Core worlds. Thus, the Border became a haven for farmers, ranchers, miners, and traders.

And fine, upstanding businessfolk such as ourselves. —Wash

With lower populations spread more evenly across the planets, the Georgia system relied less heavily on Alliance intervention. There were still governors for each world, magistrates for each moon, and sheriffs for each town, but most problems could be solved at a local level, which allowed the people on these planets a sense of autonomy from the rest of the 'Verse.

This self-reliance led many of the citizens of the Georgia system to question whether or not they needed the Alliance at all. When the Alliance decided to expand its influence over the 'Verse on a larger scale, these backwater worlds

decided to rise up, forming an Independent army. Many of the worlds in the Georgia system joined this confederacy, and many of them paid a steep price for their insurrection. *Most of us still carry those scars with us. —Zoë*

Since the end of the Unification War, the Alliance has regained control of all planets in the system and has worked to improve law enforcement and the availability of food and vital supplies. However, for some of the more heavily impacted planets, that assistance hasn't been nearly enough to restore balance. To make matters worse, some settlers have continued to reject the Alliance's aid, while others have chosen to brand themselves outlaws by intercepting supplies and selling them to the highest bidders.

Now, who would go and do such a dastardly thing? —JAYNE

With so many of the settlers in the system still holding on to their old ways, it makes Georgia an exciting—and dangerous—part of the 'Verse to visit for travelers more accustomed to the comforts of the Core!

 TIPS FOR A FUN TRIP

DO: Unwind a little. Border worlds are known for their more relaxed atmosphere and can provide a much-needed escape from the chaos of the Core. Some of the planets in the Georgia system have populations smaller than single cities on the Central Planets, so you'll have no problem finding a nice secluded place to relax.

DON'T: Unwind too much. Each Border world has its own quirks and customs, and the folks that live on them rarely take too kindly to outsiders stepping in and acting like they own the place. It's never a bad thing to get to know the locals on any planet you visit, but getting too comfortable in the Georgia system is a surefire way to get yourself into a heap of trouble.

Can't say I'll ever be comfortable out here. —Simon

And yet we still manage to find plenty of trouble anyway. —Book

? DID YOU KNOW?

- The name "Huang Long" means "yellow dragon," an ancient Chinese symbol representing the center and the element earth.

- The protostar Murphy is a helioformed brown dwarf that orbits Georgia on the outer edge of the system. Murphy has three planets that circle it.

- The orbital path shared by Georgia and the Red Sun also includes multiple Cortex relay outposts that transmit data from the 'Verse's shared communications network.

EZRA

Ezra is a rough-and-tumble border world under the thumb of a notorious gangster. For most travelers, that's enough to wipe Ezra permanently from their itinerary. But for the more adventurous set, it makes Ezra one of the most exciting stops on the Border.

 ## HISTORY AND CULTURE

The planet orbiting closest to the star Georgia, Ezra is a near-perfect example of a stereotypical Border world. Without the technological advancements of their Core counterparts, the people of Ezra struggled to transition from soldiers and refugees into new lives as farmers and ranchers. For some of them, making ends meet meant that they had to bend the law. Fortunately for them, there isn't much law to be found on the planet itself.

The only real seat of authority on Ezra floats high above it—a space station owned by infamous businessman Adelai Niska. He is said to have reached an understanding with the governing body of Ezra that allows him to operate without question or fear of prosecution. Although Niska rarely sets foot on the planet itself, his presence in the skies above is enough to keep many of the locals in line.

If I ever see that ta ma de hún dàn again... —Mal

You'll run the other way as fast as possible? —Inara

Probably, yeah. —Mal

ETIQUETTE

If you'd like to keep all of your fingers and toes on your body, it's important that you treat Ezra's locals with respect. After all, you never know who they might be working for. Offend—or accidentally harm—one of Niska's men, and you may have to answer to the boss himself.

Avoid kicking any of his thugs into your turbines. It won't go over well. —Zoë

And the engines will take weeks to clean! —Kaylee

 ## GETTING AROUND

Ezra has wide-open skies that are easy to navigate with craft of most sizes. Pilots should actively avoid the space surrounding the orbiting Niska's skyplex, however, as it is heavily armed and ready to shoot down virtually any perceived threat.

Or you could always turn off your engines and drift directly at it. —Wash

Niska's associates are known to travel to and from the space station using fast-burn rocket shuttles that allow for quick and easy travel into low orbit. These unregistered shuttles will rip right through anything in their path like a missile, so if you're planning on exploring Ezra in a personal craft, be sure to keep an eye on the skies to avoid potential collision.

 ## DINING AND NIGHTLIFE

The Groundplex: If you ever wanted to feel like a powerful gangster without actually committing any of the horrendous crimes that come with that lifestyle, then this is the bar for you. The Groundplex simply oozes opulence, with crushed velvet and gold leaf covering virtually every surface. No matter how fancy it may seem, the faux Tiffany lamps can't hide the fact that the bartenders are the real criminals, serving watered-down drinks for a premium price.

ANYONE PRETENDIN' TO BE A GANGSTER DESERVES A VERY REAL KICK IN THE JUNK. —JAYNE

REGINA

Regina is the second planet orbiting Georgia, and its entire population suffers from a rare genetic disorder. Despite their unfortunate situation, the planet's desert landscape is full of natural beauty that is certainly worth a look.

🏛 HISTORY AND CULTURE

Regina's arid deserts run rich with valuable resources, initially making this planet attractive to a slew of settlers hoping to get rich quick from mining. The deeper they dug, though, the more they discovered that Regina's resources came with a steep price.

The air underground mixed into the ore processors and created a fine dust that activated a degenerative disorder known as Bowden's Malady. This insidious disease targets a person's bone and muscle and eats away at them. Sadly, all residents of Regina—even those that have never worked in the mines—eventually develop the illness due to prolonged exposure. Bowden's is treatable with the right medicine, but it is not curable, a fact that inspires most travelers to keep their visits to Regina short.

Bowden's really is a fascinating condition. —Simon

You sure get excited by all the wrong things, don't ya, Doc. ~Kaylee

The people of Regina have risen above their affliction, proving themselves kind and hard-working. Their cities never developed like those in the Core, mostly due to the fact that a large portion of their earnings from the sale of mined resources must be used to purchase the medicine required to keep them alive. Though their frontier lives may be quaint, most of Regina's settlers are thankful they still have lives at all.

⬭ ETIQUETTE

The people of Regina live by simple rules. Treat others well and don't steal from the sick. Follow the rules and you'll be more than welcome there.

Break 'em and you'll find yourself on the worst guilt trip in the 'Verse. —Mal

⬭ GETTING AROUND

The train line that runs to many of the settlements on Regina is regularly used to transport important supplies and medicine between cities, as well as Alliance troops. However, several cars of the train are reserved for passenger travel and offer stunning views of the planet's desert landscape. The leg between Hancock and Paradiso is particularly lovely and can be a relaxing and romantic way to celebrate any special occasion. Trains run continuously throughout the day. Tickets are available at local stations.

Anyone up for another honeymoon? Captain? —Zoë

▶ TIPS FOR A FUN TRIP

DO: Bring spare meds. While the citizens of Regina usually have access to the medication they require to combat Bowden's Malady, occasional shortages and thefts lead to sudden escalations in the disease's symptoms among the populace. If you can afford some Pescaline D, bring it with you and donate it to families less fortunate than you.

DON'T: Sell spare meds. Helping the sick out of the goodness of your heart is the right thing to do. Helping the sick so you can make a profit is not. When Pescaline D is in low supply, it's not uncommon for visitors to try to make a fortune by selling marked-up meds to desperate residents. That despicable act will also land you in a jail cell if the local sheriff discovers your schemes... and the longer you stay locked up, the more likely you'll need those meds for yourself!

Remember, kids: Stealing from people in need is BAD. —Wash

Yet stealing from anyone else is somehow perfectly acceptable? —Book

Now you're catchin' on, shepherd! —Mal

BOROS

Boros may be a Border Planet, but it has an unusually high Alliance presence. For those willing to follow the rule of the law, this planet is a great place to make a fresh start beyond the often oppressive confines of the Core.

 ## HISTORY AND CULTURE

Boros is Georgia's third planet and features a nice balance of industry and agriculture, offering opportunity to just about anyone who chooses to migrate there. That fact has made Boros a frequent destination for those who need a break from the daily grind of life in the Core.

If the transport ship you hired ever gets you there... –Simon

While the pace of life there may be a bit more easygoing than on the Central Planets, Boros doesn't share the same level of unchecked freedom that some of its neighboring Border Planets enjoy. This is due to a large Alliance contingent present on the planet keeping a watchful eye on its citizens, especially those who have recently arrived.

Perhaps it's better we never arrived... –River

 ## ETIQUETTE

Boros remains one of the most popular destinations for travelers who want to experience the thrill of a Border world, while still staying safely under the protection of Alliance forces. Attitudes on Boros are more relaxed than in the Core, but still a bit more reserved than on other Border worlds. Find the right balance and you'll fit right in.

🛍 SHOPPING AND ENTERTAINMENT

Sanchez Ship Repair and Storage: If your engine has stopped humming or your hull's been breached, you can count on this family-owned maintenance bay to get you cruising the black again in no time flat. Because of their mechanical know-how, no-questions-asked mentality, and affordable rates, the Sanchez brothers have become favorite repair techs for crews of all varieties. If you're planning on settling down on Boros, they also offer storage hangars that can discretely accommodate ships of virtually any size or legal status.

They may know their way 'round a ship, but they ain't layin' hands on my girl! —Kaylee

🍸 DINING AND NIGHTLIFE

The Unification Bar: This tap house is a favorite among Alliance cadets stationed on Boros for training. Decorated with military memorabilia from the Unification War, the bar was designed specifically to boost the morale of trainees after a long hard day of drills, appealing to their patriotic nature with a wide assortment of potent drinks named for famous battles (be sure to try the Du-Khang daiquiri). Of course, the list of libations may have also been designed to remind any remaining Independents on the planet exactly who emerged victorious from battle.

Someone oughta show these purple bellies what a real soldier looks like! —Mal

KERRY

Few worlds are as painfully mediocre as Kerry, the fourth world in the Georgia system. While there may be nothing wrong with this small Border world, there's not a whole lot right with it either. One visit and you'll surely be asking, "Can we go now?"

 ## HISTORY AND CULTURE

Kerry is a Border Planet that often gets overlooked by travelers for its sheer averageness. Its natural features are pleasant, but not exceptionally beautiful. Its people are hospitable, but not overly friendly. Its climate is tepid, and its culture is unmemorable. It's the kind of destination where you could dock a dozen times but never really remember what you did there or why you bothered.

If you really want to know what Kerry is like, just visit any other Border world, ignore all of the things that make it unique and interesting, and you'll have a pretty good idea.

It's easy for many to ignore the beauty found in the average. —Simon

Tell me about it! —Kaylee

 ## SIGHTS AND ACTIVITIES

Madcap: Kerry may be as dull as they come, but the planet's sole moon, Madcap, is quite the opposite. Although the moon earned its name from its erratic weather patterns that shift without warning, it is also a popular destination for adrenaline junkies from across the 'Verse. If you've got deep enough pockets, you can buy just about any sort of thrill on Madcap, from cyclone surfing to atmo-diving. If you're pregnant or have a heart condition, though, you're probably better off just staying on Kerry.

That sounds more like it! Can we go? Now?!? —Wash

ITHACA AND PRIAM

Ithaca and Priam are binary planets, two worlds revolving around each other as they share an orbital path around Georgia. Though these dual worlds may be linked by their proximity, they could not be more different from one another.

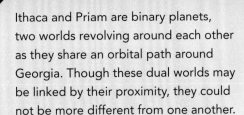

Like if a stuffy doctor had a sister who was a psycho mind assassin? —Jayne

You mean a psycho mind assassin who knows where you sleep? —River

 ## HISTORY AND CULTURE

When settlers first arrived on Ithaca and Priam, the two worlds were not all that different from any other Border world. But as some settlers made their fortunes off the hard work of others, a cultural divide grew between the wealthy and the working class. It wasn't long before Priam's elite started buying up huge swaths of land to create massive estates, forcing those who toiled in their fields and factories to relocate to neighboring Ithaca.

The rift between the two worlds reached its peak during the Unification War when the downtrodden citizens of Ithaca rebelled against their neighbors on Priam. The Alliance stepped in to aid their industrial partners on Priam, while the Browncoats sent a small number of troops to help defend Ithaca's citizens and their meager assets. Though casualties were kept to a minimum, the wounds created between these worlds still run deep in the forms of travel bans and trade embargoes.

DINING AND NIGHTLIFE

Twin Worlds Brewery: Before Ithaca and Priam were irrevocably ripped apart, the early settlers proudly worked together to produce a number of high-quality goods that were shipped throughout the 'Verse. Because of the rift between classes, most factories were shut down or relocated to other worlds with better relationships between workers and management. One product, a 'Verse-favorite beer known as Ithaca/Priam Ale—or IPA— has recently returned to production on Ithaca in a new brewery now wholly owned by workers from the brand's original Priam facility. Tours and samplings are available on Fridays and Saturdays. Valid IdentCard required.

I'd be a lot more enthused about supportin' the plight of the workin' man if the stuff didn't taste like xióng mao niào. —Mal

PROPHET

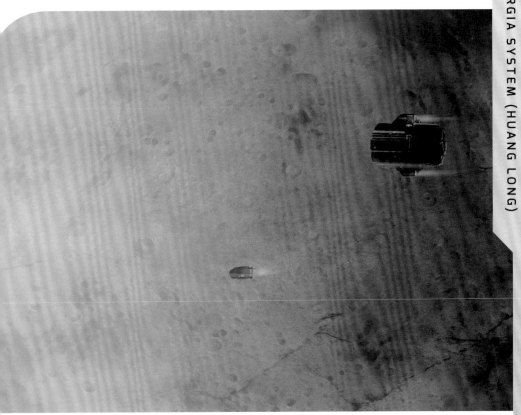

Circling in the sixth orbital path of the Georgia system, Prophet and its moons, Perdido and Dunny, are currently scheduled for terraforming.

HISTORY AND CULTURE

Prophet is one of three planets in the Georgia system that has yet to be made habitable. Although the terraforming process is usually funded exclusively by the Alliance, a conglomerate of wealthy business owners on Priam has provided additional sponsorship for Prophet's terraforming. It is said that, once terraforming is complete, the world will be opened exclusively to a new wave of workers for Priam's factories, essentially eliminating any leverage that the people of Ithaca may have held over their closest neighbor.

Prophet is scheduled to be habitable by 2530, with its moons following shortly after.

'Verse has already got enough scars. It don't need a planet of scabs. —Mal

ELPHAME

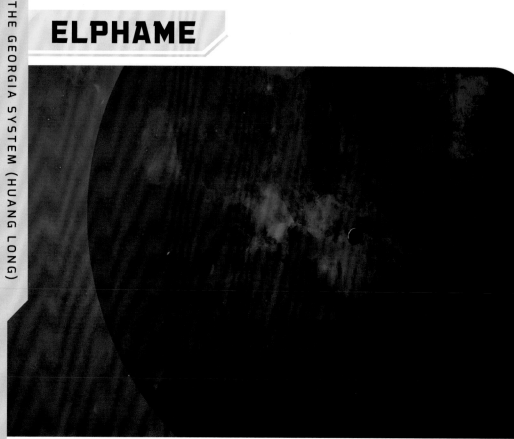

Elphame is a gas giant with four tiny moons that circle its enormous body. Though small, these moons are serene and lovely, which has made them a popular final destination for many seasoned travelers nearing the end of their days in the 'Verse.

 ## HISTORY AND CULTURE

While Elphame itself may not be a habitable planet, its four tiny moons were thoughtfully designed to capture the epitome of comfortable living for the 'Verse's elderly inhabitants. *And you thought there would be scabs on Prophet... —Wash*

Summerhome and Sweethome are both retirement moons that cater to every need of their aging clientele. The major difference between the two moons is simply aesthetic. Sweethome bears a closer resemblance to the Core, while life on Summerhome is similar to that on a Border or Rim world. While one may feel more like "home" to different residents, both moons offer the same exceptional level of care.

No use payin' extra to die out on the Border. It'll gladly kill ya for free. —Zoë

Dedicated caregivers are on call at all hours, but the support staff and medical technicians actually make their permanent homes on another moon, Ithendra. Teams arrive via shuttle and serve weeklong shifts on one of the retirement moons before swapping out with another crew.

 ## SIGHTS AND ACTIVITIES

Fiddler's Green Memorial Moon: The final moon of Elphame, Fiddler's Green, is reserved for those who have reached the end of their journey. This cemetery moon is said to be one of the most peaceful places in the 'Verse and is the resting place for many of the system's most important historical figures. Fiddler's Green is open for visitation from dawn until dusk, but strict noise ordinances are always in effect. *WHEN I die, just float my body out into the black. —JAYNE*

We may not even wait that long. —Mal

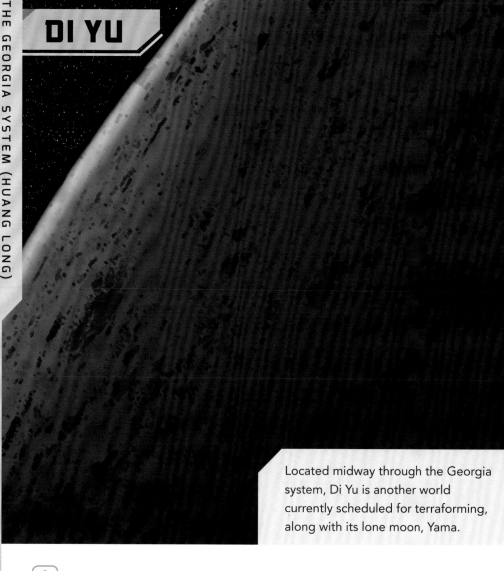

DI YU

Located midway through the Georgia system, Di Yu is another world currently scheduled for terraforming, along with its lone moon, Yama.

 ## HISTORY AND CULTURE

Out on the Border, all eyes have been on Di Yu for some time now, due primarily to the fact that the planet's centrally located orbital path offers easy access to virtually every other world circling Georgia. While the Alliance has not yet shared specific plans for the planet post-terraforming, there have long been rumors of shifting increased Alliance Navy assets into the Border, and a planet in Di Yu's prime location would be the perfect place to create a remote command outpost.

Di Yu is scheduled to be habitable by 2565, with its moon following shortly after.

Just what we need. More Alliance ships muckin' up our airspace. —Zoë

I suspect they feel the same way about us. —Book

ATHENS

Athens holds the ninth spot in Georgia's orbit and was profoundly affected by the Unification War. Once the gleaming capital of the system, Athens was forced to take an unexpected step backward before forging ahead in new directions more in sync with other Border worlds.

In other words, it was bombed into submission. —Zoë

 ## HISTORY AND CULTURE

The capital of the Georgia system, Athens was one of the few planets in the Border to develop cities as impressive as those found in the Core. Sadly, few of those cities—including the people that called them home—survived the Unification War intact. Since the war, Athens has become more like its neighboring Border worlds, with a stronger focus on farming and ranching.

Athens has four frontier moons: Anooie, Argabuthon, Ormuzd, and Whitefall. Before the war, these satellites seemed quaint and perhaps even a bit backward compared to the planet that they circled. Now, however, there isn't much of a difference between them . . . except for the fact that the moons have fewer defenses and are far more vulnerable to raiding parties.

Good to know . . . for a friend . . . —JAYNE

65

While the Alliance helps to rebuild the infrastructure on Athens, the planet's moons have been left to their own devices. That has allowed ambitious residents to buy up large swaths of land, thus creating their own rule of law. If you plan on visiting any of these lands—particularly Whitefall—be prepared to defend yourself and your possessions from those who feel they have the right to stake claim to anything that touches down in their territory.

And be sure to say 'Hi' to Patience for us. Then take cover. —Mal

ETIQUETTE

On Athens, keep your head down. Hard work is valued over all else, and proving you can do your part of a job earns respect.

On Athens' moons, keep your guns drawn. The settlers there don't care about hard work, they only care about what they can take and who they have to shoot to get it. If you've got something worth fighting for, you'll likely have to do just that.

Hell, even if you ain't got somethin' worth fightin' for, chances are you'll have to do it anyways. —Mal

SIGHTS AND ACTIVITIES

Quad-Moon Cattle Drive: The four moons of Athens are known for their ranching operations, and travelers looking to experience the rustic life of a cowhand for themselves can sign on to help move herds between moons. There's nothing quite like riding across the desert plains on horseback to clear your mind . . . or to make you appreciate your life back in the Core. And when the time comes to load those cattle into your ship's cargo hold, you're in for one of the biggest challenges of your life!

They forget that they're cows in there. —River

DAEDALUS

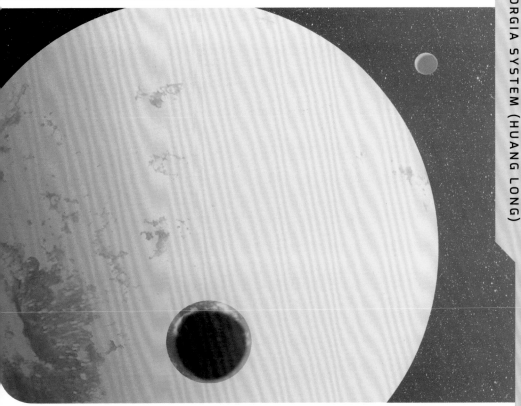

The moons of Daedalus, the second gas giant in the Georgia system, are wholly owned by the Blue Sun Corporation and used for the manufacturing of molded protein—a versatile, shelf-stable foodstuff commonly enjoyed by crews on long voyages across the 'Verse. *"Enjoyed" isn't exactly the word I'd use. —Wash*

 ## HISTORY AND CULTURE

Much like the nearby Elphame, Daedalus is a gas planet without any habitable surface. Its moons—Arvad's Helm, Notterdam, Rea, and Box—have become the primary production chain for a staple in every traveler's diet, molded protein.

The first moon, Arvad's Helm is where research and development takes place. New flavors are developed to keep those endless journeys across the black a bit more exciting. *I am not sure that "red" can technically be considered a flavor. —Simon*

Notterdam is where large-scale cultivation of the protein occurs, though the process is a highly classified trade secret, and outside visitors are strictly prohibited.

The third moon, Rea, is a factory world where the raw protein is heavily processed, preserved, and molded into its final form.

Finally, the appropriately named moon, Box, serves as the packaging and shipping center to deliver the product across the 'Verse.

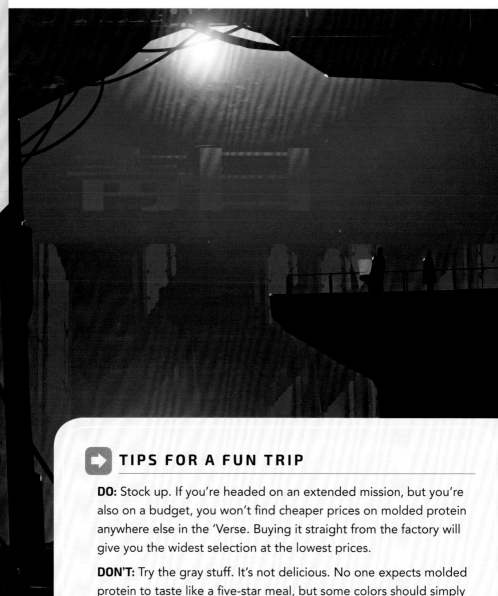

TIPS FOR A FUN TRIP

DO: Stock up. If you're headed on an extended mission, but you're also on a budget, you won't find cheaper prices on molded protein anywhere else in the 'Verse. Buying it straight from the factory will give you the widest selection at the lowest prices.

DON'T: Try the gray stuff. It's not delicious. No one expects molded protein to taste like a five-star meal, but some colors should simply be outlawed. Gray molded protein proudly bears the label "Original Recipe," which should make you very glad that the team on Arvad's Helm has since come up with other, more palatable options.

But, boy, is it great for patchin' up busted hydraulic lines! ~Kaylee

NEWHOPE

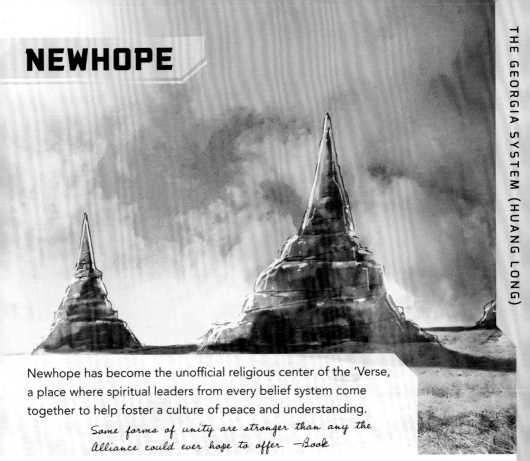

Newhope has become the unofficial religious center of the 'Verse, a place where spiritual leaders from every belief system come together to help foster a culture of peace and understanding.

Some forms of unity are stronger than any the Alliance could ever hope to offer. —Book

HISTORY AND CULTURE

New Hope was originally settled by a prominent group of Buddhist monks that left Sihnon when the planet became a bit too crowded for their tastes. Word got out about their sanctuary world, and other religious leaders began to make pilgrimages to Newhope to experience the planet's serene beauty firsthand. It wasn't long before they made Newhope their home as well. In a 'Verse still scarred from a struggle for independence, Newhope is proof that we can all coexist peacefully. *We're plenty peaceful... in between the shootin' at folks. —Mal*

SIGHTS AND ACTIVITIES

Newhope Cultural Center: This multidenominational temple was built atop one of the planet's tallest mountains and hosts services for over a dozen different faiths in multiple languages every day. The center was completely funded by personal donations and has no direct ties to the Alliance. An adjoined party center is available to rent for weddings and other festivities.

Maybe they could throw River an exorcism. —Jayne

We all have our demons, son. —Book

'cept you, right, Shepherd? —Kaylee

If you only knew, my child... —Book

69

THREE HILLS

A planet whose sole industry is commerce, Three Hills is the best possible place to go when you're searching the 'Verse for an impossibly hard-to-find item.

OR if you're lookin' to unload goods that might be LESS-THAN-legal. —JAYNE

Like, oh, I don't know, a vintage Earth-That-Was laser pistol prototype. Hypothetically speakin', of course. —Mal

 ## HISTORY AND CULTURE

In its earliest days, Three Hills was home to a monthly flea market, where vendors from across the 'Verse could come and peddle their wares. When crowds from the Core to the Rim started making regular trips, organizers realized that the market should become a permanent fixture. As the number of vendors increased, the market spread to cover virtually the entire planet.

Instead of cities, Three Hills is divided into shopping districts, each focusing on a different type of product—from clothing and jewelry to replacement ship parts to ancient artifacts. If it's been made, it can be bought or sold on Three Hills . . . and that includes extremely rare items that may have been acquired in an unlawful manner. In fact, it's said that the only thing more impressive than the markets on Three Hills is the planet's black market.

Found my toy dinosaurs here! —Wash

And I've made him stay on the ship every visit since. —Zoë

? DID YOU KNOW?

- Rare collectibles that survived from Earth-That-Was fetch top dollar. This is the perfect place to sell that dusty antique for a premium price.

- All vendors on Three Hills are expected to obtain proper licenses from the Trader's Guild, a policy nearly impossible to enforce thanks to the millions of sellers who have set up shop here.

- One of Three Hills' moons, Conrad, has the highest population density in the 'Verse, thanks to its pleasant climate, beautiful landscapes, and proximity to Three Hills' markets.

MEADOW

Located near the outer edge of the Georgia system, Meadow is another world currently scheduled for terraforming, along with its moons, Salyut and Mir.

 ## HISTORY AND CULTURE

Before Meadow was scheduled for terraforming, it was not uncommon for deep-space salvage companies to use the planet's surface as a scrapyard for large-scale debris that they didn't want to risk bringing into atmo on a populated planet. That practice was put to an end after it drew an influx of scavengers into the Georgia system and stretched Alliance resources on the Border even thinner than usual. Now, dumping scrap on Meadow has been outlawed, and crews have begun disassembling and removing any remaining debris as they prep the planet to undergo the terraforming process.

Meadow is scheduled to be habitable by 2560, with its moons following shortly after.

Sure do miss that scrapyard. Lots of great memories in those wrecks. —Kaylee

HERA

The first of three planets circling the protostar Murphy, Hera was once a thriving agricultural hub that linked the Core, Border, and Rim. Its strategic location made Hera a crucial battlefield during the Unification War, directly resulting in the planet's decline.

 ## HISTORY AND CULTURE:

Before the Unification War, Hera was just another world on the Border, known for the export of its agricultural abundance. That changed after the Battle of Serenity Valley, though, when the Alliance's bombs blackened the planet's skies. Hera was no longer able to grow enough crops to sustain the planet's own citizens, so the planet's economy collapsed more quickly than the Independent army. *Okay, who wrote this gorramn book?!? —Mal*

With farming out of the question, the people of Hera have turned to mining the rich ore beneath the ground. The transition has been slow, though, and it may take decades before Hera can fully recover from the fallout.

Now that sufficient time has passed, a rising interest in the Unification War has also created a burgeoning tourist industry that has brought swarms of 'Verse history buffs to Hera to experience the majesty of Serenity Valley firsthand.

Already had that honor the first time, thank you very much. —Zoë

ETIQUETTE

Hera is a somber planet that carries the weight of history. No matter whether you support the heroic Alliance or the ill-fated Independents, when visiting Hera's hallowed grounds, it is only proper to show the utmost respect to all who fell here.

 ## SIGHTS AND ACTIVITIES

Serenity Valley: Though this rocky canyon may not seem all that spectacular at first glance, its significance to the 'Verse is far greater than it appears. It was in this valley that Independent forces held their ground against Alliance soldiers for seven weeks in one of the greatest—and bloodiest—battles of the Unification War. The Battle of Serenity Valley crushed the Independents and led to their ultimate surrender . . . but not before a combined 500,000 fighters from both sides of the fray lost their lives on this spot. The hills of Serenity Valley are now lined with their graves. Tours are available daily, except on holidays.

Do you ever think of going back there, Captain? –Simon

No need. Still see it every time I close my eyes. —Mal

 ## SHOPPING AND ENTERTAINMENT

Boneyards: After the aforementioned Battle of Serenity Valley, Hera became a graveyard for more than just soldiers who fought in the Unification War. It also became the final resting place for an impressive assortment of ships and other military equipment. Unlike the soldiers, though, many of the vehicles still stand a chance of being brought back to life with enough love and care from a dedicated crew. A number of local businessmen have bought up the land where these ships crashed, creating enormous boneyards filled with vehicles in various states of spaceworthiness. If you're looking for a cheap ride—and don't mind rebuilding a catalyzer or two—the salvage yards on Hera are the place to go.

This here's where you found Serenity, Captain... so not every memory's a bad one! ~Kaylee

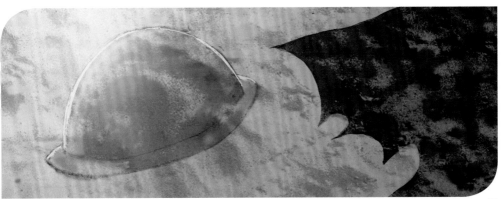

DINING AND NIGHTLIFE

Browncoat Bar and Grille: This popular dining spot just a few miles outside of Serenity Valley celebrates the rich history of Hera. Its menu draws inspiration from the agricultural bounty that the planet produced before the Unification War, though many of the ingredients are now shipped in from other planets, thanks to the effects of post-war pollution on crop cycles. Portions are surprisingly large, so you may find yourself surrendering before you can finish—just like the Independent soldiers who gave this local eatery its name.

I'm serious. Someone find out what planet this piece of gou shi was published on... and load up on ammo... —Mal

APHRODITE

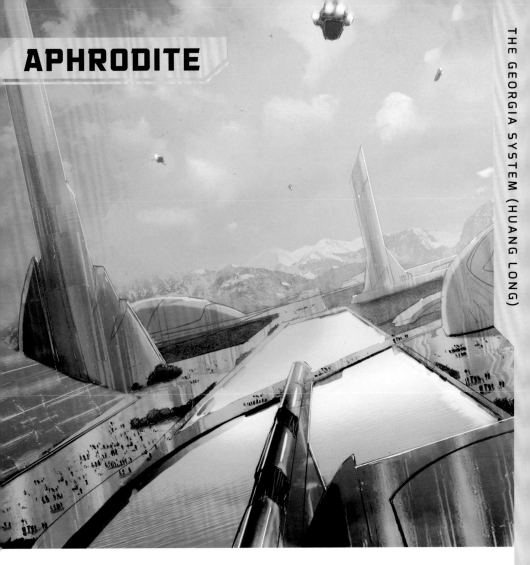

The second world orbiting Murphy, Aphrodite stood apart from surrounding worlds during the Unification War, a choice that had positive consequences on its status in the 'Verse but a distinctly negative effect on its standing in the Border.

 ## HISTORY AND CULTURE

Aphrodite gets its name from an ancient goddess of love, which seems extremely appropriate when you consider this world's stance during the Unification War. Unlike the settlers on its neighboring worlds, Hera and Shadow, the people of Aphrodite opted to abstain from combat. This turned out to be a wise choice, as the planet is the only one of Murphy's three worlds whose ecosystem and economy were not gravely impacted as a result of the brutal conflict.

You cannot fault one for choosing a path of peace. —Book

We most certainly can. —Zoë

In fact, since the conclusion of the war, Aphrodite has thrived thanks to increased Alliance funding. Improvements in infrastructure have attracted a greater number of visitors from the Core, but that has earned Aphrodite the disdain of most other Border worlds.

who needs honor and individual freedom when you can have better roads and ports? —Zoë

Cowards and sellouts, every one of 'em. —Mal

I have had countless requests from clients on this world, but the Captain refuses to dock there. —Inara

These spineless traitors wouldn't know how to treat a lady if they saw one. —Mal

🍸 DINING AND NIGHTLIFE

Venus: This nightclub in Aphrodite's capital city of Paphos is a great spot to have a cocktail and look for love. Its signature drink is a potent play on the ancient elixir of the gods, ambrosia. A few of these and you'll believe that you're looking down the bar at Aphrodite herself. That may not be the case, however, as an unfortunate quirk in the terraforming process has greatly increased the viability of the Y chromosome in settlers, making the majority of children born on Aphrodite male. The current gender ratio among citizens is five men to every one woman, so if you are looking for love with a local lady, best to get to the bar early!

How sweet. —Inara

Not even a whore. —Mal

Never mind. —Inara

SHADOW

Shadow was once a glorious prairie world with crops sprawling as far as the eye could see. Now, it is a barren blackrock that serves as a constant reminder that peace on the 'Verse often comes at a high cost.

Home sweet home. —Mal

 ## HISTORY AND CULTURE

Shadow is the third planet orbiting the protostar Murphy, making it the furthest world from the center of Georgia system and, on occasion, the closest to either the Core or the Rim. In terms of its culture though, Shadow is clearly closer to the Rim than the Core.

Lacking in grand cities or structured government, Shadow instead thrived thanks to its vast plains that were used for growing grains and raising cattle. Most settlers on Shadow came there specifically for the freedom it granted, so when the Alliance attempted to unify the planets, it was no surprise that Shadow was one of the first worlds to stand against the idea. Their defiance did not go unanswered.

Still wouldn't have changed a thing. —Mal

The Alliance bombed Shadow mercilessly, leaving an uninhabitable rock in their wake. Those who survived left the planet to find a new homestead or to fight back against the Alliance in the Unification War. Since the fall of the Independent army, there has been no attempt to recolonize Shadow. Now, the silent world serves as a solemn warning to any who might choose to stand against the Alliance.

And a constant reminder of why we must. —Zoë

? DID YOU KNOW?

· Shadow was only habitable for around one hundred years. Terraforming was completed on the planet in the early 2400s, and it was rendered unlivable by 2511.

· It is said that the origin of the signature browncoat uniform of the Independent army can be traced to the dirt-colored trench coats commonly worn by the farmers on Shadow.

· Shadow's three moons are still sparsely populated, mostly by refugees from the planet itself. After surviving the Alliance's attacks, they refused to move to any planet where their so-called "oppressors" would control their destinies.

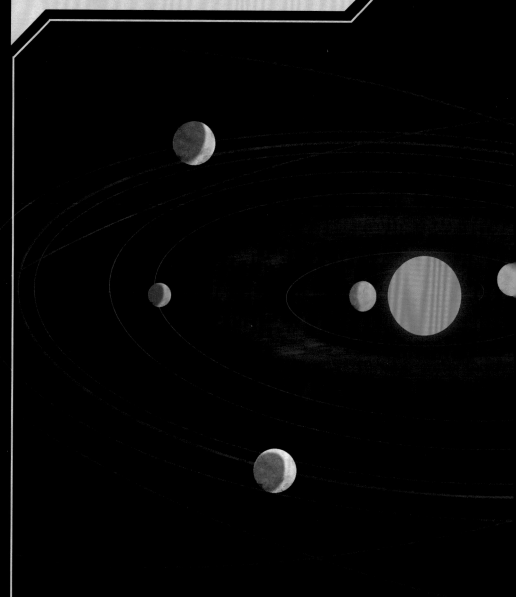

THE RED SUN SYSTEM (ZHU QUE)

On the exact opposite side of Bai Hu from Georgia, but sharing the same orbital path, is the Red Sun system. Although these two systems are forever separated by a great distance, the similarities between the Red Sun's planets and those circling Georgia are significant. Zhu Que may be smaller and cooler than its orbital partner, Huang Long, but its worlds are just as important in giving the Border its inimitable flavor.

🏛 HISTORY AND CULTURE

When people think of the Border, they immediately conjure up images of dusty plains and weathered farmhands moving cattle or tilling fields. Like its fellow Border system, Georgia, the Red Sun system has plenty of worlds that fit that picture perfectly. However, while the majority of Georgia's planets fall under the stereotypes associated with the Border, the Red Sun system offers a bit more diversity in its destinations. From the churning seas of New Melbourne to the icy peaks of St. Albans, the Red Sun system's varied landscapes appealed to settlers who were interested in more than just crops and livestock.

But what could be better than cows and corn? Oh, yeah... everything. —Wash

Like all worlds in the 'Verse, the Red Sun's assortment of terraformed planets and moons are ruled by the Alliance. However, because this system played a much smaller role in the Independent rebellion that led to the Unification War, the Alliance has been more relaxed in its oversight and has been more likely to let disputes be solved by local governors and magistrates. While this does allow each planet to chart its own course a bit more freely, it has occasionally led to increased corruption, especially when a magistrate lets power go to his head.

Still, if you're looking to experience the full gamut of what the Border has to offer, the Red Sun system contains the widest variety in the smallest space. While you might find that Georgia's planets and moons start to blur together after just a few stops, there's no mistaking the unique worlds surrounding the Red Sun.

Some of us prefer blendin' in to standin' out... least until it suits us otherwise. —Mal

👕 WHAT TO WEAR

Because the Red Sun is a smaller, colder star, planets in the Red Sun system experience temperatures that average about ten degrees cooler than their Georgian counterparts, so be sure to bring some warmer clothes when you visit this system. There are still plenty of scorching deserts on a number of Zhu Que's planets, but those who have frequently visited Georgia will likely find the climate in this Border system far more tolerable.

❓ DID YOU KNOW?

· The name "Zhu Que" means "red phoenix," an ancient Chinese symbol representing the south and the element fire.

· The protostars Himinbjorg and Heinlein are helioformed brown dwarfs that orbit the Red Sun on the outer edges of the system. The worlds that circle these two protostars account for more than half of the Red Sun system's planets.

· The floating Cortex outposts that travel along the same orbital path shared by Georgia and the Red Sun link back to a massive Cortex hub hosted on the planet Aesir.

JIANGYIN

The planet closest to the Red Sun is a world where there are more cows than people. The settlers who do live on Jiangyin, however, are always happy to see a new face arrive on their secluded little world . . . so happy, in fact, that they might never let you leave!

Important information that might have come in handy before our visit. —Simon

 ## HISTORY AND CULTURE

Despite its vast plains perfectly suited for raising livestock, Jiangyin is one of the most undeveloped and backward planets on the Border. Only a few small towns are scattered across this planet's barren landscape, and those tend to be occupied by ranchers not too different from those you'd find on any other Border world.

Should you decide to wander beyond the towns and head toward the hills, though, you'll encounter settlers unlike any in the 'Verse. These humble hill folk have carved out meager lives on the outskirts of civilization. Unfortunately, their lives are so hardscrabble that they are occasionally forced to take what they need from those who visit the planet. Sometimes that means supplies, other times it can even mean people!

As River and I managed to learn firsthand. —Simon

Make sure your fellow travelers are aware of your location at all times when on Jiangyin, in case you find yourself an unexpected guest of one of these groups. The Alliance has kept a safe distance from this unpredictable world, and local law enforcement is too busy tracking down outlaws and cattle rustlers to care about the whereabouts of a few misplaced off-worlders.

So you best hope to be travelin' with some big damn heroes. —Zoë

 ## ETIQUETTE

When in Jiangyin's towns, behave as you would on any Border world. As long as you respect local law and refrain from any criminal dealings, you should be able to have a pleasant visit.

Or at least one that doesn't end with you getting shot. —Book

If you encounter those who dwell in the hills of Jiangyin, remember that they tend to be primitive and superstitious. Because they are easily frightened by things that don't fit into their way of life, it can make them quite dangerous. Their lack of understanding of the worlds beyond their own have reportedly led to frequent unprovoked attacks on unsuspecting outsiders.

Otherwise, they were quite nice. –River

They were insane! –Simon

No more than you or I. –River

THAT AIN'T SAYIN' A WHOLE lot. –JAYNE

 ## SIGHTS AND ACTIVITIES

Spring Festival: When they aren't busy herding cattle (or kidnapping tourists), the people of Jiangyin are often found throwing festivals to celebrate a number of seasonal events. A favorite among the younger settlers is a springtime dance that takes place on the outskirts of town. Beneath a tent draped over a sacred tree, the unwed locals, identified by white sashes, twirl together to lively music in hopes of finding a perfect partner. If you're a new settler on Jiangyin, expect to be the belle of the ball, as no one on this little world wants to court their own cousin.

I imagine this applies to any world, not just Jiangyin. –Wash

SHOPPING AND ENTERTAINMENT

The Post-Holer: Most travelers don't come to a planet like Jiangyin to shop, but if you happen to be on the planet anyway, this little supply store is a hidden gem. Although its shelves of canned food and rusty tools may seem no different than those sold at any other shop on any other Border world, the store also offers a wide array of crafts made by local artisans, including china plates, handmade rag dolls, and wooden sculptures of generic waterfowl, all of them made with care.

And longing. (And it was a swan, by the way.) ~Kaylee

 ## TIPS FOR A FUN TRIP

DO: Show your strength. The hill folk of Jiangyin may be willing to randomly abduct you, but only if you look like an easy target. If you possess powerful weapons and seem to be a threat to their way of life, they will likely be too terrified to do anything but let you go free.

DON'T: Show your skills. Travelers with in-demand abilities, like doctors and teachers, are at the greatest risk of abduction. After all, the people of Jiangyin only take what they need, and what they usually need is help from someone more educated than they are. If you do possess valuable talents, keep a low profile and stay aware of your surroundings at all times.

That means stop your showin' off, Doc. ~Zoë

Duly noted. ~Simon

NEW MELBOURNE

Vastly different from most other Border worlds, New Melbourne is an aquatic planet with limited habitable landmass. Those who make their home on the second planet in the Red Sun system are more interested in sailing the seas than the stars.

🏛 HISTORY AND CULTURE

For those who have grown weary of the dusty, dry planets populating the Border, New Melbourne offers a unique escape thanks to the fact that a large majority of its surface is covered in water. Although habitable land does exist on New Melbourne, one rarely comes to this planet to explore it. Instead, New Melbourne is a common destination for those searching for adventure on the high seas. *Or for treasure beneath them. —Jayne*

The settlers on New Melbourne have made their living off the ocean that surrounds them. Most work actively as fishermen, and those who aren't actually catching fish are working at processing plants to prepare fish for export to other planets.

ETIQUETTE

Citizens of New Melbourne tend to be somewhat abrasive toward outsiders. Some claim that the salt water has hardened their veins, but the truth may be far simpler—they don't view anyone who isn't navigating the open seas as a "real" captain. And they may be on to something, as the comfort of a hermetically sealed cockpit and the smoothness of the black are no match for the unforgiving wrath of the open ocean. Show respect or you're likely to find yourself marooned. *I'll show 'em a real Captain. —Mal*   *where'd you manage to find one of those, sir? —Zoë*

GETTING AROUND

If your vessel has docked for repairs or refueling, the only real way to get around New Melbourne is by charter boat. These services can be hired via the Cortex and are ready to take you on a scenic tour of the New Melbourne coastline (or straight to land if your stomach can't handle the waves).

WHAT TO WEAR

An external layer of waterproof clothing is recommended on New Melbourne. Not only will it prevent you from becoming soaked by sea spray, it will also create a boundary between you and the overwhelming fishy smell that permeates everything on the planet.

No matter what you wear, you'll smell like that planet for weeks. —Wash   *For some members of our crew, that would be a welcome improvement. —Inara*

DINING AND NIGHTLIFE

Red Sun Wharf: While restaurants on the Core planets may treat seafood as a delicacy, on New Melbourne it's at the center of every meal. Every port on this planet has its own local pub that serves fried fish alongside a nice cold pint of beer, but few match the quality of the Red Sun Wharf in New Melbourne's capital city. Their trademark battered cod is tender and flaky and is perfectly complemented by a salad of locally cultivated algae. With a fresh ocean breeze blowing in off the patio and live entertainment seven nights a week, a visit to the Red Sun Wharf is a true sailor's delight.

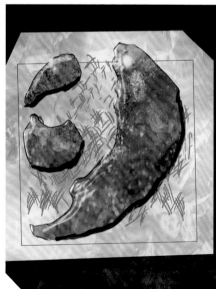

GREENLEAF

Greenleaf is one of the most appropriately named planets in the 'Verse. Covered in lush vegetation, this jungle world is the point of origin for many of the system's most vital medications, as well as some of its most notorious smugglers.

 ## HISTORY AND CULTURE

Thanks to its tropical climate and abundance of gorgeous rainforests, Greenleaf is rapidly becoming a popular destination for travelers across the 'Verse. Those forests provide far more than just a stunning vacation setting, though. The rare plants grown on Greenleaf are the source of many of the medicines prescribed throughout the 'Verse, from Pescaline D to Hydrozepam.

Sounds like we might have better luck here next time you wanna play master criminal, Doc. —Zoë

The planet's abundant resources attracted pharmaceutical companies, who first set up harvesting operations on Greenleaf. Soon, they found it more cost effective to build their processing plants here, as well as medical facilities to run drug trials, providing a boost to the planet's economy alongside a rise in their own profits. Approximately 85 percent of Greenleaf's settlers now work for these medical companies in some capacity.

Unsurprisingly, we've only dealt with the other 15. —Inara

Many of those who choose not to work for these pharmaceutical giants still make their money from the production of these medications. Some process their own crude versions of the drugs from illegally acquired crops, while others take an easier route and steal shipments from the planet's ports and sell them on the black market at a steep markup. This surge in criminal activity has attracted the attention of the Alliance, who had all but ignored Greenleaf in the past.

WHAT TO WEAR

A lot of the planets on the Border are hot, but Greenleaf adds an extra layer of uncomfortable humidity to the mix. With all the dangers in the jungle though, protection from the elements is a must. Make sure to wear thin, breathable fabrics that can shield your body from harm while still keeping you cool. And be sure to bring an extra set of clothes to replace the ones you're bound to soak through with sweat. *Such high humidity does quite a number on my hair . . . —Book*

Thank you for the warning. I'll stay far away. —River

DINING AND NIGHTLIFE

The Greenleaf Tavern: The jungle vegetation on Greenleaf can be used for far more than medicinal purposes. The planet produces a wide variety of exotic, edible plant life rarely found on any other planet in the 'Verse. This has inspired some of the system's more adventurous chefs to migrate here for a chance to experiment with the fresh and flavorful flora. One popular bistro, the Greenleaf Tavern, has a menu that is in constant rotation based solely on what the chef finds blooming along the road on his journey to work each morning.

Let's hope he steers clear of the opium fields. —Simon

LET'S HOPE HE DOESN'T. —JAYNE

TIPS FOR A FUN TRIP

DO: Escape the heat. Greenleaf's oppressive climate can quickly become overwhelming to travelers used to more temperate worlds, so you might be better off keeping your visits short and retreating to a nearby moon. For those who can't tolerate the temperature, there are plenty of affordable lodging options on the working-class moon called Dyton.

That is, if you can tolerate the accents. —Mal

DON'T: Trim the bushes. Although the flora on Greenleaf may seem to be growing wild and free, some species of medicinal herbs are actually genetic hybrids developed by the planet's pharmaceutical companies. If you're caught with even a small clipping of one of these proprietary plants, it could turn your green thumb red-handed.

HARVEST

Named for the abundance of produce it once supplied to the 'Verse, Harvest has faced a decades-long drought that has forced its citizens into dire straits. With the planet's arid soil unable to cultivate crops, the mud on one of its moons has now become Harvest's most valuable resource.

Now here's a place that seems mighty interestin'! —Jayne

Here we go again . . . —Mal

 ## HISTORY AND CULTURE

The fourth planet orbiting the Red Sun was once home to the most plentiful fields in the system, but a severe drought struck the planet and led to a rapid decrease in production. Harvest never truly recovered, and many of the former farmers were forced to seek work elsewhere. Not all of Harvest's settlers were quite so eager to give up, however, and those that remained have adapted to grow crops that require little moisture—such as certain grains and legumes—in an effort to earn back their planet's appellation.

One of Harvest's two moons, formerly known as Piltdown, was renamed Higgins' Moon in honor of its magistrate, who discovered that this satellite's soil was the perfect chemical composition to create high-quality ceramics. Thanks to the efforts of thousands of slaves and indentured servants, this mudball of a moon has now become the best place in the 'Verse to get this lightweight, ultra-strong material, which can be found in virtually every ship sailing the stars.

Sounds like a delightful place, this Higgins' Moon. —Jayne

No. No, it doesn't. —Simon

ETIQUETTE

Harvest, like most Border worlds, is full of hardworking individuals who don't much care for the interference of outsiders who might threaten their relative freedom.

Most of the residents of Higgins' Moon, however, are well aware that freedom is not a luxury they possess. They serve their magistrate out of necessity, not choice, and have relied on outsiders to step in to perform acts of rebellion that they are unable or unwilling to carry out themselves. As evidenced by the local folklore, it doesn't take much to become a legend here.

I find their choices in heroes downright inspirin'! —JAYNE

No surprise there... —Kaylee

 WHAT TO WEAR

If you're visiting Higgins' Moon, be sure to bring some extra clothes. You might be able to wash out the mud, but it's unlikely you'll ever be able to wash out the pungent odor that hangs heavy in the moon's air. *It smells like glory! —JAYNE*

And fèi fèi de pì yan. —Zoë

 SIGHTS AND ACTIVITIES

Canton Factory Settlement: We all know how mud is made: Take dirt and add some water. But the workers at the Canton Factory Settlement show that something as simple as digging for mud can become a real art form. Not only do these "mudders" harvest the mineral-rich soil, they also work at the factories that turn it into ceramic bricks that are shipped throughout the system to be shaped into functional components. Custom-forged ceramic parts can also be ordered with advance notice (and significant down payment). A gift shop with ceramic figurines and souvenir mud boots is located just outside the main processing plant.

Got me my own teeny tiny JAYNE. —JAYNE

So I've heard. —Inara

DINING AND NIGHTLIFE

Mudslingers: A favorite of the workers at the Canton Factory Settlement, this rustic saloon may be the perfect place to escape after a long hard day of shoveling mud, but it also happens to serve one of the most uniquely intoxicating brews this side of the Rim. It's no surprise that locals spend their few hard-earned dollars on this potent fermented beverage known as "Mudder's Milk," which is packed full of carbohydrates, vitamins, protein, and, of course, plenty of alcohol. Live musicians play on weekends, but they tend to play variations of the same folk ballad about the "Hero of Canton" over and over.

No use strayin' from the classics. —JAYNE

Order an extra round and you might be lucky enough to pass out before the fifth chorus. —Wash

? DID YOU KNOW?

· Local legend claims that the aforementioned Hero of Canton was a man named Jayne. It is said that he robbed the rich magistrate and then selflessly showered the stolen money down onto the town below as he flew off into space.

· A statue of the Hero of Canton once stood in the center of the Canton Factory Settlement, but it was reportedly knocked down by Jayne himself when he returned to save his devoted followers a second time. The head of the statue now hangs over the bar at Mudslingers.

· Though the people of Canton will tell you otherwise, Jayne is typically a girl's name. *Told you so. —River*

ST. ALBANS

After visiting one too many dry and dusty planets on the Border, a stop on St. Albans offers the perfect chance for travelers to cool down. Though it may look like nothing more than a frozen wasteland on the surface, visitors always warm up to the Red Sun's frosty fifth planet.

HISTORY AND CULTURE

Notorious for being one of the coldest planets in the 'Verse, St. Albans is covered in snowcapped mountain ranges that stretch high into the heavy clouds that fill the sky. Strong, bitter winds whistle through the canyons, forcing the planet's population centers into the low-lying valleys that offer a bit of extra protection from the elements.

Although some might think that a world with these conditions is best left unsettled, the rich ore deposits on St. Albans proved to be worth the general discomfort of subzero winters. And while the citizens of St. Albans have adapted to thrive in the planet's colder climate, visitors are never quite prepared for the intense chill awaiting them when they step onto this frozen wonderland.

This place feels colder than the black itself. — Mal

ETIQUETTE

The settlers of St. Albans are a kind and family-oriented people who are welcoming to strangers and are quick to show warmth, even in the coldest areas of their planet. However, they are also fiercely protective of their own, and will band together against any outsider they view as a threat. Unlike many of the rugged Border worlds surrounding it, on St. Albans, kindness is the key to a pleasant stay.   *A shame Tracey strayed so far from home . . . —Zoë*

 ## WHAT TO WEAR

The forecast for every day on St. Albans is snow, so be sure to dress warmly. Multiple layers of heavy knit fabrics are recommended, with as little exposed skin as possible, especially around the head and ears. Bright colors will also help you stand out if you get lost in a whiteout.   *Apparently, your mother read this book, too, Jayne. —Wash*

 ## DINING AND NIGHTLIFE

Ice Planet Emporium: One of the 'Verse's favorite treats, the delicious frozen novelty on a string known as the ice planet was created on St. Albans. Though these spherical snacks are now sold on the streets of spaceports across the system, none of those icy imitations can quite compare to the originals crafted using ice carved straight from the cliffs of the planet itself. Although you're likely to find a local spin on this classic in each of St. Albans' settlements, the Ice Planet Emporium is by far the most famous parlor, with locations across the planet and dozens of exotic flavors offered. Try their signature Cayenne Planet for the perfect mix of ice and spice!

Delicious . . . but confounding. —River

 ## LODGING

Local inns are available on St. Albans, but they may not have enough blankets to keep your toes from going numb. You might be better off parking your ship in one of the many caves found in the planet's mountainous regions. Not only do these caverns offer privacy and protection from the elements, but staying in your ship will save you enough credits to stock up on extra ice planets for the journey home. (Don't forget a cryo chamber to keep them from melting!)

You can use mine. —River

ANSON'S WORLD

The sixth planet in the Red Sun system, Anson's World is a popular stop for explorers with courageous spirits who wish to share their knowledge of the 'Verse with fellow travelers. The information accumulated here has helped to shape the 'Verse as we know it.

 ## HISTORY AND CULTURE

Anson's World is dedicated to research and understanding of the 'Verse. The planet is home to the Universal Cartographic Information Society, an autonomous group of explorers and mapmakers dedicated to charting the far corners of the 'Verse. While the Alliance may get the credit for populating the far reaches of the 'Verse with habitable worlds, many of those worlds may not have been discovered if not for the tireless efforts of the surveyors stationed here.

 ## SIGHTS AND ACTIVITIES

And in some cases, we would have been better off. —Zoë

History of the 'Verse Guided Tours: Anson's World is the launching point for a series of tours dedicated to exploring the history of the 'Verse and its unique cultures in depth. Climb aboard a Series 4 Firefly and learn about the planets and their histories from a UCIS certified historian. Tours are currently available for the White Sun and Red Sun systems, but due to popular demand, operations are expected to expand to include Georgia and Kalidasa in the near future. A tour circumventing the entire 'Verse has long been rumored but is not currently planned due to the considerable time and resources required for such a journey.

We'll take you on the same trip for half the price. —Mal

But there's no guarantee you'll make it back alive. —Simon

Fine. A quarter then. —Mal

93

JUBILEE

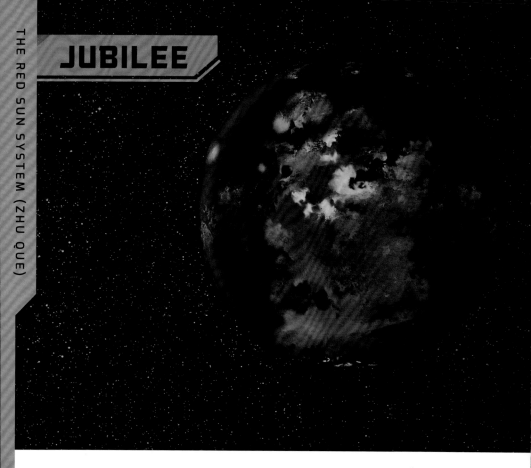

Jubilee is the seventh planet in the Red Sun system. Along with its moon, Covenant, Jubilee is currently scheduled for terraforming.

 ## HISTORY AND CULTURE

After the Unification War ended, some members of Alliance leadership began to explore how they could prevent conflicts in the future. Upon study, they realized that truly integrating the Alliance into Border worlds meant far more than sending in troops and enforcing laws. It meant building bridges between cultures and reminding settlers from all corners of the 'Verse that they had started in the same place. To that end, once Jubilee's terraforming completes, it will be home to the first museum that celebrates the history of the 'Verse's Border worlds. This Alliance-funded project will allow visitors to record their personal stories and include them in an archive available to all future generations of settlers.

Jubilee is scheduled to be habitable by 2550, with its moon following shortly after.

I've got some stories to share . . . —Mal

Not sure they're the kind the Alliance is lookin' for, Captain. —Zoë

AESIR

The first world orbiting the protostar Himinbjorg, Aesir is a Border Planet where something slightly unusual is farmed and mined: data. This pristine world is home to the servers that feed the 'Verse-wide information network known as the Cortex.

HISTORY AND CULTURE

Most of us take the Cortex for granted. As long as we can remember, it's just been there, providing us an entire universe worth of knowledge with the touch of a button. No matter where we are in the 'Verse, the Cortex is with us. Yet we rarely stop to think about where the Cortex itself is actually located.

Based on some of the things I've accidentally stumbled across on the Cortex, I'd prefer not to know. —Wash

Aesir is the perfect planet to house the sensitive equipment required to store and relay the millions of zettabytes of data that populate the Cortex's mainframes. Although close to its protostar, temperatures on Aesir are surprisingly moderate, and the world's humidity and pollution levels are extremely low. Cool breezes blowing over the world's oceans provide a natural cooling effect to prevent servers from overheating.

Because of the delicate nature of the Cortex network and the information it stores, Aesir is highly restricted to travelers without high-level Alliance security permits. The planet is populated primarily by technicians who keep the Cortex up and running at all times. They work tirelessly to make sure that every world—from the wealthiest planet in the Core to the smallest moon in the Blue Sun system—always has access to the most powerful thing in the 'Verse: knowledge.

"Lips that speak knowledge are a rare jewel." Proverbs 20:15. —Book

? DID YOU KNOW?

· The majority of Aesir's surface is covered in water, and its surface area is made up of nine major islands, including its capital, Asgard.

· Each island on Aesir has been specialized to focus on a different aspect of maintaining the Cortex, from coding to hardware repairs. They are all directly linked by high-speed relay stations floating in the planet's oceans.

· Aesir's moons—Bestla, Borr, and Odin—are each equipped with powerful transmitters that broadcast to the orbiting relay stations floating throughout the 'Verse.

MOAB

Moab is the second world circling Himinbjorg. Along with its moons, Red Rock and Mesa, Moab is currently scheduled for terraforming.

 ## HISTORY AND CULTURE

As more planets and moons are terraformed and settled, the 'Verse's natural resources are being consumed at an alarming rate. Fortunately, some of the worlds still waiting to be processed will provide additional supply sources for important materials and alleviate a bit of the strain on existing operations. One of those pending worlds, Moab, is known to contain huge deposits of durable stone—such as granite, marble, and sandstone—that can be excavated and shipped to neighboring worlds to be used in the construction of buildings and monuments. Though Moab is nowhere near ready for habitation, prospectors are already staking claims on quarry sites.

Moab is scheduled to be habitable by 2531, with its moons following shortly after.

This sounds like one world we really might want to take for granite. —Wash

I married this man. Of my own free will. —Zoë

BRISINGAMEN

Brisingamen is a small, unassuming planet traveling around Himinbjorg in its third orbital path. Tucked between two uninhabitable worlds, Brisingamen is easy to overlook, but those who visit this planet quickly discover that it is literally the Red Sun system's hidden gem.

 ## HISTORY AND CULTURE

From its sparkling oceans to its sun-drenched mountaintops, the colors on Brisingamen seem to shine a little brighter—and there's a good reason for that. This small planet is the 'Verse's leading exporter of quartz and other rare gemstones. *"To hell with knowledge. Just gimme the RARE jewels." —Jayne*

The crystals mined on Brisingamen are more than just beautiful, they're also useful. Raw crystals are shipped across the 'Verse where they are cut and processed for a variety of purposes, from powering portable electric generators to decorating the necks of the wealthiest socialites.

To occasionally filling the hidey holes in our cargo bay. —Zoë

 ## LODGING

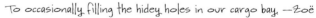

Crystal Palace: A resort on Brisingamen's first moon, Freya, the Crystal Palace was built as a place of healing and rejuvenation for the body, mind, and spirit. Built entirely of raw quartz and silicate stones mined on the planet below, the expansive spa supposedly taps into the natural energy contained within the crystals to realign guests' chakras and restore their centers. As one might suspect, a number of expensive spa treatments are available, and personal healing crystals can be purchased for an additional fee in the gift shop.

Ain't no one puttin' nothin' anywhere near my chakras. —Jayne

THE RED SUN SYSTEM (ZHU QUE)

ANVIL

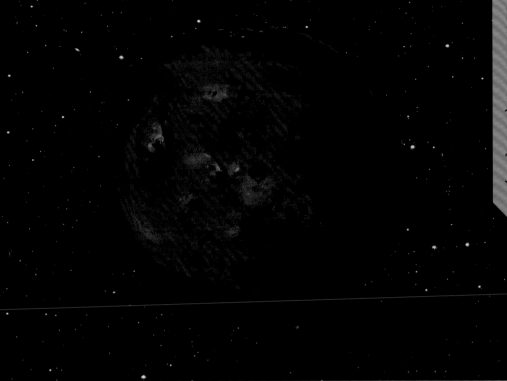

Anvil is the fourth and final world orbiting Himinbjorg. Along with its moon, Hammer, Anvil is currently scheduled for terraforming.

HISTORY AND CULTURE

As is the case for the nearby world of Moab, terraforming is scheduled to begin on Anvil in the immediate future. Anvil is a world with an exceptionally hot core that frequently releases flows of liquid ore onto the planet's surface. Far more volatile than most other terraformed worlds, it is uncertain whether the terraforming process will be able to satisfactorily stabilize the molten rivers running beneath Anvil's crust to produce a world suitable for habitation. However, should the process succeed, the sheer amount of valuable metal already detected on this hostile world will guarantee a rapid influx of settlers willing to brave the heat as they dig their way to fortune.

Anvil is scheduled to be habitable by 2532, with its moon following shortly after.

We'll have to add this to our calendar. —Mal

written as if you actually believe any of us will live that long. —Zoë

TRIUMPH

Visiting Triumph, a quaint little world near the edge of the Red Sun system, is like taking a step backward in time. This isolated planet is not widely recognized as a tourist destination, but a quick visit here could offer you a completely different perspective on the 'Verse. *And a completely different marital status, I'm told. —Simon*

 ## HISTORY AND CULTURE

The first—and smallest—of the four celestial bodies orbiting the protostar Heinlein, Triumph is similar to many Border Planets in that it lacks most cutting-edge conveniences. The major difference, however, is that the settlers on Triumph deliberately chose to shun modern advancements and higher education in order to live a simpler life free of excess and temptation.

Oh, there's still a fair amount of temptation. —Wash

Triumph's settlements are governed by pious elders who put God's will before that of their people. This has unfortunately allowed travelers of the far-less-holy variety to take advantage of the peace-loving populace on countless occasions. Despite their vulnerability, the settlers of Triumph still find a way to revel in the extraordinarily ordinary life that they chose.

Best beware revelin' with 'em, though, right? —Kaylee

 ## ETIQUETTE

The settlers of Triumph are a highly religious people who take great joy in celebrating their faith via a number of archaic ceremonies. Unfortunately, because their contact with the outside world is limited, they have a tendency not to realize the importance of explaining the significance of those ceremonies to guests. While you certainly don't want to offend your hosts, it doesn't hurt to ask a few questions about regional customs. Depending on what town you're in, a few extra steps could mean the difference between a festive dance and a sacred ceremony!

GETTING AROUND *I've always warned the Captain to pay more attention to the fine print . . . —Zoë*

Most of the settlers on Triumph have spurned fancy flying ships and have instead adopted more primitive means of travel, such as the stagecoach. Procuring one of these traditional horse-drawn wagons can be a romantic way to get a better view of the planet's unsullied countryside, not to mention a great way to move supplies and personnel from one settlement to the next without drawing too much attention from the locals. Bandits, however, are another story.

WHAT TO WEAR

Due to Triumph's proximity to Heinlein, the sun can get quite intense. It is recommended that travelers wear light fabrics that allow for maximum airflow, as well as some sort of head protection to combat the protostar's powerful rays.

A pretty floral bonnet would do quite nicely. —JAYNE

SHOPPING AND ENTERTAINMENT

Maiden House: While certified Companions may be widely respected throughout the 'Verse for their wide range of skills and knowledge, the young women on Triumph are not nearly as fortunate when it comes to their schooling. Most girls never attend school at all, but those that the elders deem the most pleasing to the eye are sent off to the Maiden House and taught one thing—how to serve their future husbands. Once they have learned their role, these obedient brides-to-be are then sold or traded in return for necessary goods and services. Although arranged relationships may seem strange to outsiders, these young women are all of consenting age, and the majority take pride in keeping Triumph's traditions alive. If you have limited luck in the way of romance, a visit to the Maiden House might be your best chance to find the devoted partner you've been seeking.

Or an impeccably trained con artist looking to take you and your crew for all they're worth. —Inara

You all got that out of your systems now? Good. Moving on . . . —Mal

PAQUIN

Unlike its solitary neighbor, Triumph, Paquin is one of the most visited planets in the Red Sun system. The second world orbiting Heinlein is well known throughout the 'Verse as a hotspot for arts and culture that attracts travelers and settlers alike.

🏛 HISTORY AND CULTURE

Paquin began as a commune of nomadic settlers who traveled to the Border to more freely pursue their unique creative endeavors. Word spread about their experimental forms of performance, attracting other like-minded artists from all over the 'Verse. Each new group that arrived brought with them new forms of music, dance, theater, painting, and sculpture from their own home worlds, which spanned from the most sophisticated Core planets to the untamed edges of the Rim.

Over time, Paquin's art scene went from underground to mainstream. Thanks to investments from some of the Border's most powerful citizens, a proper theater district was constructed. Local artists now show their works in

It's where I first learned all about yarbling. —Wash

What's that? —Simon

Honestly? I haven't got a clue... —Wash

multimillion-credit galleries instead of tents. Tourists flock to Paquin from all over the 'Verse to find the next hot cultural trend long before it ever reaches the Core.

At its heart, however, Paquin is still a world of nomads, and it is the constant arrival of new artists from distant worlds that continues to fuel the planet's unmatched creative energy. Of course, not every new arrival is able to make their dreams of stardom come true, which often leads to desperate situations as they struggle to survive. Which means Paquin has earned as much of a reputation for its crime rate as it has for its sublime culture.

RATHER BE A THIEF THAN AN ARTIST. LEAST MY MAMMA CAN STILL LOOK ME IN THE EYE. —JAYNE

🛍 SHOPPING AND ENTERTAINMENT

Paquin Interplanetary Opera House: On the shore of Paquin's capital city, Wagner, sits the centerpiece of the planet's theater district. This majestic building is the permanent home of the Zhu Que Opera and the Heinlein Orchestra, both of which are renowned throughout the 'Verse for their willingness to take on the most challenging classical works as well as innovative new pieces by aspiring local composers. When the space is not being used by either group, it is rented for a greatly reduced fee to local theater troupes who cannot afford their own stages. Performance information is available on the Cortex or at the box office.

A night of culture might do this crew some good. —Inara

Nothing reforms us heathens like a fat lady singing in a metal bra. —Mal

Actually, that don't sound half bad . . . —JAYNE

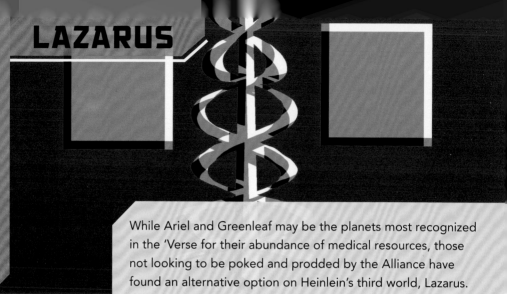

LAZARUS

While Ariel and Greenleaf may be the planets most recognized in the 'Verse for their abundance of medical resources, those not looking to be poked and prodded by the Alliance have found an alternative option on Heinlein's third world, Lazarus.

 ## HISTORY AND CULTURE

Despite its lack of high-tech hospitals and pharmaceutical factories, Lazarus is a planet wholly dedicated to healing. In its earliest days, Lazarus was designated as a "quarantine world"—a place where settlers from other planets with contagious illnesses could be sent to live out the rest of their days in peace without the risk of infecting others. However, it was soon discovered that a number of serious maladies began to go into remission with no viable medical explanation—just being on Lazarus seemed to improve the health of the planet's sickest citizens.

Intriguing. I would love to learn more. —Simon

Sure wouldn't mind bein' quarantined with you, Doc. —Kaylee

Trained doctors and scientists from the Core have tried time and again to quantify any healing properties the planet may have, but to no avail. Even without concrete answers, hope alone has been enough to keep a steady stream of pilgrims flocking to Lazarus for a renewed chance at life.

Sounds like a bunch of NEW-AGE mumbo jumbo to me. —JAYNE

Never underestimate the healing power of faith. —Book

 ## WHAT TO WEAR

If you're not on Lazarus to be healed, try to avoid exposing yourself to anyone who is—which is just about everyone else. Protective gear with a self-contained oxygen system—such as a space suit—is recommended at all times and should be thoroughly decontaminated before reentering your ship to ensure that you don't bring home a highly contagious souvenir. If you do find yourself unexpectedly ailing, however, at least you're in the right place to correct it. As they say, a few extra weeks on Lazarus never killed anyone.

Another key world on the Border, Silverhold is the last planet orbiting Heinlein and the outermost planet in the Red Sun system. While its citizens may not be very wealthy, the work done on Silverhold is essential to the economy of the 'Verse.

 ## HISTORY AND CULTURE

Like many other planets on the Border, Silverhold was originally founded as a mining world, thanks to an abundance of metal discovered beneath the planet's surface. While most other planets contained ores that could be reshaped into ships and skyscrapers, the metals found on Silverhold were of a far more precious variety.

Despite the plentitude of wealth buried beneath this planet's surface, those that dwell here tend to live simple lives with no frills. Most workers owe a great deal to the mining companies that control the land, and they slave each day simply to pay for food and board. Any abuses to the workers' rights are usually overlooked, thanks to notoriously corrupt Alliance officers who patrol the Silverhold colonies and are rumored to take bribes from the mine owners to look the other way. *You ever run across a lieutenant named Womack, you give him our regards . . . followed by a swift punch to the jaw. —Mal*

 ## SIGHTS AND ACTIVITIES

Silverhold Mint: These days, most travelers pay for their daily expenses with electronic credits, but real money still exists in the 'Verse—in fact, some Border Planets still only accept physical credits for purchases. Since Silverhold is where most of the raw materials required to strike coins are found, it made sense for the Alliance to build their casting facility here as well. If you don't mind paying money to see money, tours are available and include admission to a museum of rare credits from throughout the history of the 'Verse. Unfortunately, no free samples are available on the tour. *Just because they ain't givin' 'em away don't mean you can't just take 'em. —Jayne*

THE KALIDASA SYSTEM (XUAN WU)

Just beyond the Border lies Kalidasa, a star whose worlds are the first to be considered part of the Rim. While the planets surrounding Georgia and the Red Sun may seem undomesticated to most travelers, the Kalidasa system offers more adventure, more variety, and far fewer rules.

Sounds a bit closer to our speed. — Wash

HISTORY AND CULTURE

Kalidasa is a yellow star similar in size, color, and brightness to Georgia. It is orbited by more planets than any other star in the 'Verse. However, not all of those worlds are habitable, since Rim worlds were not a first priority for terraforming.

Although the Rim and Border do not have a physical boundary between them—such as the Halo asteroid belt that divides the Core and the Border—they are separated by an orbital path that is home to six Alliance deep-space stations. These floating cities are used as command posts for Alliance operations in both the Border and the Rim, as well as refueling posts for Alliance Navy patrol vessels.

Despite the nearby Alliance outposts, settlers on the Rim aren't much for regulations. They wouldn't have ventured this far from the Core if they were looking for the Alliance to tell them what to do. The Alliance tends to agree, substantially limiting the amount of manpower, funds, and resources allocated to Rim worlds. This has led to worlds on the Rim that are a bit more experimental than those found in the Border. If the Border is the 'Verse's frontier, then the Rim is the untamed wild beyond, and the people who live there like it just fine that way.

The Rim's kinda like the Doc's moonbrained sister. Ya might think you can handle her, but she could prob'ly kill ya in a dozen different ways 'fore ya blink. —JAYNE

At least two dozen. —River

The lack of regulation on the Rim has also led to more pollution, more crime, and more danger throughout the Kalidasa system. In fact, while nearly every terraformed planet and moon in the Core and Border has something worthwhile to offer to travelers, there are a few worlds in the Kalidasa system that we recommend avoiding altogether.

If you're more comfortable in a somewhat stable, predictable environment, it's best not to venture beyond the Border. If you crave excitement and don't mind a bit of peril, then Kalidasa has plenty of each to spare.

? DID YOU KNOW?

· The name "Xuan Wu" means "black tortoise," an ancient Chinese symbol representing the north and the element water.

· The protostar Penglai is a helioformed brown dwarf that orbits Kalidasa midway through the system.

· Kalidasa has three gas giants—Heaven, Zeus, and Djinn's Bane—the highest number of any system in the 'Verse.

SHO-JE DOWNS

The first planet orbiting Kalidasa is home to one of the 'Verse's most notorious illegal gambling rings. But that's not the only underground scene on Sho-Je Downs, as the intense heat from the nearby sun has driven most settlers below the planet's surface.

HISTORY AND CULTURE

Sho-Je Downs looks unimpressive from the surface—nothing more than a hot, barren world with few signs of life. But it's beneath the planet's surface that the action is really happening. To escape the scorching rays of Kalidasa, settlers here have taken advantage of the planet's naturally porous substratum and populated an elaborate network of tunnels and caverns below ground.

Most of the caverns are dedicated to sustaining their inhabitants' daily life, with extensive areas devoted to the growth of moss and fungi crops. But some of the deeper hollows are accessible only to those willing to pay a steep entry fee.

There, high rollers can place their bets on virtually anything—from simple hands of Tall Card to brutal gladiator-style arena battles. But be careful. If you try to cheat the house, you might find yourself suddenly going from betting on a death match to participating in one. *Sign me up. —JAYNE* *Gladly. —Mal*

🗑 SHOPPING AND ENTERTAINMENT

Sho-Je's Down: One of the planet's moons, Miyazaki, is a fantastical world full of quirky inhabitants and unusual traditions. One of the principle forms of recreation involves the juggling of the planet's most abundant species of bird, the goose. While most geese are fortunate to simply be tossed about by the locals, others are plucked of all their feathers, which are then used to create some of the finest comforters in the system. These blankets are not often used in the high-temperature environments on Miyazaki or Sho-Je Downs, but they have become highly coveted throughout the 'Verse and go for top dollar on colder planets, like St. Albans. *Spent six weeks here. Goslings were juggled. —Wash*

VERBENA

Not all of the Rim worlds are capable of thriving on their own. On some worlds, like Verbena, the same settlers who looked to escape the influence of the Alliance soon discovered that creating a sustainable way of life without a bit of help isn't nearly as simple as it sounds.

 ## HISTORY AND CULTURE

The settlers who came to Verbena, the second planet in the Kalidasa system, did so with the same intent of any other group who moved to the Rim—to forge their own path in the 'Verse without having to answer to outside forces. It wasn't long, however, before they learned the hard truth that the barren rock they chose to be their home wasn't about to let them have their way so easily. The dirt wouldn't grow many crops and the rocks beneath weren't of much value either.

Rather than abandoning the planet, the settlers swallowed their pride and called in help from the same governing body they sought to escape. The Alliance gladly answered Verbena's call, funding the construction of factories to manufacture gear shifts and other parts for their patrol cruisers. This allowed the citizens of Verbena to earn a living wage, while providing the Alliance far cheaper labor than they would find on more established worlds. While it might not have been the arrangement the settlers wanted, it was the choice they had to make to ensure that Verbena survived. *Better to die free, if you ask me. —Mal*

No one did. —Inara

 ## DINING AND NIGHTLIFE

Verbena Factory Fairs: When a new factory opens on Verbena, it is common for the local citizens to hold a fair to celebrate the occasion. Similar to most other traveling carnivals found throughout the 'Verse, these fairs entertain locals with unique performers, games of chance (significantly more legal than those found on Sho-Je Downs), and deep-fried foods.

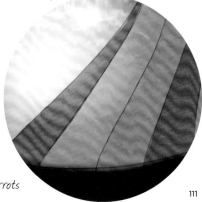

Ooh! I hope they have some of those curly carrots I've heard so much about! —Wash

CONSTANCE

The third planet in the Kalidasa system, Constance is a simple world where religion is a part of everyday life. It's a welcoming world that rarely turns away a visitor—a form of kindness that gets its citizens into more trouble than it's worth.

 ## HISTORY AND CULTURE

Religion has always been a part of Constance. The planet was originally settled by a small sect of dedicated priests and nuns who sought sanctuary from the temptations of the Border. As they soon found out, being isolated out on the Rim isn't exactly conducive to keeping vows of celibacy. To avoid the early extinction of their colony, they continued to devote their spirits to the Lord while making a few small exceptions about their bodies.

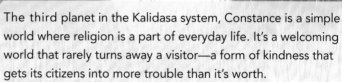

Maybe them priests just got tired of not gettin' nun. —Jayne

I pray for your soul, boy. —Book

I have a strange feeling you might be wasting your time, Shepherd. —Wash

The settlers' descendants kept the religious traditions at the heart of Constance alive, fostering a world built on benevolence and virtue. Visitors to Constance are embraced and treated with kindness and charity, a situation that many less pious travelers have attempted to use for their personal gain.

 ## TIPS FOR A FUN TRIP

DO: Attend a sermon. The church is the centerpiece of each settlement on Constance, and it can be humbling to witness a community so devoted. Visitors are often asked to participate in the daily sermons to provide unique perspectives.

DON'T: Betray their kindness. Though they might preach peace and love, the citizens of Constance don't like to be swindled. They have been known to chase those who take advantage of them out of town with pitchforks!

Anything to liven up a boring day at church! —Mal

GLACIER

Glacier is the fourth planet in the Kalidasa system. Along with its moon, Denali, Glacier is currently scheduled for terraforming.

 ## HISTORY AND CULTURE

The first of five planets in the Kalidasa system still waiting to be terraformed, Glacier has a layer of ice surrounding its surface so thick that it's hard to determine where the actual planet begins. The addition of an atmosphere during the terraforming process will likely increase the planet's temperatures significantly, causing much of the world's nonpolar ice to melt away and providing the planet with an abundance of fresh water. Unfortunately, should the temperatures continue to rise beyond optimal levels, sea levels will follow suit, putting Glacier's habitability at risk. To avoid this, terraforming crews are considering exporting large volumes of water and ice to neighboring worlds in need of extra moisture, including the soon-to-be-terraformed Vishnu.

Glacier is scheduled to be habitable by 2570, with its moon following shortly after.

VISHNU

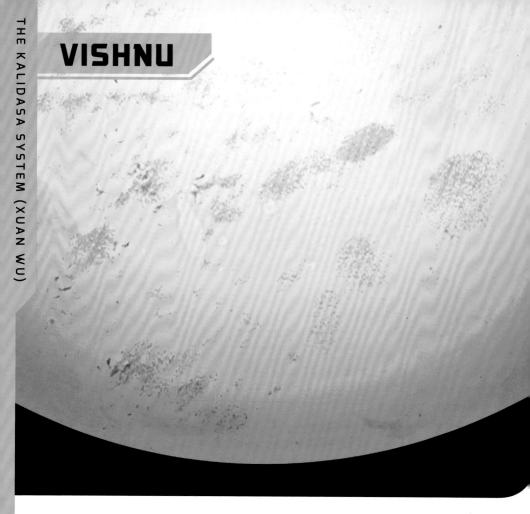

The fifth world orbiting Kalidasa, Vishnu and its moons—Ganesha and Rama—are also uninhabited and currently scheduled to undergo terraforming.

 ## HISTORY AND CULTURE

Though similar in size to nearby Glacier, Vishnu's native state couldn't be more different than its ice-covered Kalidasan companion. Temperatures on Vishnu run high, with plumes of hot steam rising from volcanic vents that cover the planet's bone-dry surface. Surveyors have discovered rivers of scalding hot water flowing beneath the surface of the planet, which could prove beneficial during the terraforming process. If needed, crews might rely on the surplus of ice found on Glacier, transporting it to Vishnu's surface in order to reduce temperatures and add extra moisture to the environment.

Vishnu is scheduled to be habitable by 2550, with its moons following shortly after.

HEAVEN

The first of three gas giants in the Kalidasa system, Heaven has fewer moons than either of its counterparts. But as they say, quantity isn't nearly as important as quality . . . but unfortunately, the moons of Heaven haven't got much of that either.

At least we ain't the only ones. —Mal

 ## HISTORY AND CULTURE

With a name like Heaven, you might expect the habitable moons that circle this planet-sized ball of gas to be some of the loveliest in the 'Verse. And perhaps they were before settlers reached them and spoiled their natural beauty, treating their new home worlds as if they were completely disposable. Once the trees were chopped down and the resources were used up, all that was left were four overcrowded and overpolluted worlds with little left to offer.

The outermost moon, Tilottama, was the first of the moons to be settled. Once it was stripped clean, the majority of its people migrated inward, to Rambha, then to Menaka, and finally, to Urvasi. With nowhere left to go after that, most of the population has learned to live on Urvasi despite its inhospitable conditions, though many dream of someday finding the stars somewhere beyond the smoke that fills their skies.

Some days I really miss these moons. Then I take a big deep breath of clean air and, nope, not so much. —Wash

 ## LODGING

Heaven's three outer moons are littered with empty settlements, abandoned by the locals when they moved on to other more habitable worlds. As such, there are plenty of structures on these moons that a down-on-their-luck traveler could use as temporary free lodging. Of course, there's always the chance that someone else with the same idea got there first, so before you get comfy, make sure you really are alone.

Might be fun to visit the place where my husband grew up. —Zoë

Sure, if you can find it underneath the layers of soot. —Wash

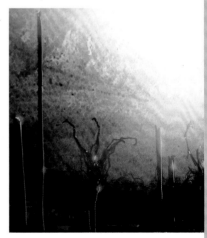

ANGEL AND ZEPHYR

Like Ithaca and Priam in the Georgia system, Angel and Zephyr are two neighboring planets that share the same orbital path around Kalidasa. But while Ithaca and Priam are at constant odds with each other, Angel and Zephyr live in perfect harmony.

Aww! Ain't that sweet? Like the 'Verse's very own Wash and Zoë! ~Kaylee

 ## HISTORY AND CULTURE

The small worlds of Angel and Zephyr seem quite different at first glance. Angel is an industrial world, home to manufacturing facilities the size of cities, while Zephyr is an agricultural society with a focus on growing crops and raising livestock. Yet it was the disparities between these two planets that made them perfect partners. What one world needs, the other produces, creating a symbiotic relationship unlike any other in the 'Verse.

If you plan to visit either Angel or Zephyr, try to schedule in an extra day to experience the adjacent planet. Whether you're an Alliance advocate or a hardcore Independent, the long-standing spirit of collaboration between these worlds may give you a fresh perspective on how the rest of us can peacefully coexist.

Perhaps even this crew could learn a thing or two from them. —Book

🛍 SHOPPING AND ENTERTAINMENT

A–Z Outposts: This popular chain of supply stores originated on Angel and Zephyr as an easy way for settlers on these two sister planets to exchange goods. The A–Z Outposts on Zephyr deal mostly in Angel's manufactured products, while those on Angel are fully stocked with produce and meats cultivated on Zephyr. The chain has recently begun to expand to other planets on the Rim, selling items produced on both Angel and Zephyr.

DELPHI

Circling Kalidasa in the eighth orbit, Delphi is currently being prepped for terraforming along with its three moons, Clio, Thalia, and Calliope.

HISTORY AND CULTURE

Delphi is another of the Kalidasa system's uninhabited planets, but this world already has a purpose for when the terraforming process is complete. According to Alliance officials, Delphi has been selected to serve as a dedicated repository for the 'Verse's most important historical texts, including many that survived from Earth-That-Was. While some have scoffed at the idea that such a significant installation would be built out on the Rim rather than close to the Core, the Alliance is said to see the Delphi project as another key step toward the unification of the 'Verse.

Delphi is scheduled to be habitable by 2530, with its moons following shortly after.

The Alliance can try and take my freedom, but ain't no one gonna force me to read! —Jayne

Hey, I'm not even sure they could teach you to read. —Wash

NEW KASMIR

Nearly identical in size to Earth-That-Was, New Kasmir is a planet whose fragrant breezes and endless bounty belie the fact that its fields once ran with blood as red as the planet's signature apples.

Yum? —Wash

 ## HISTORY AND CULTURE

Since it was terraformed, the planet of New Kasmir has been primarily known for its orchards capable of producing copious amounts of fruit—including peaches, cherries, and several varieties of citrus. But by far, the most famous (and delicious) of New Kasmir's crops is its apples. It is said the planet has over a hundred different varieties of apple that vary in flavor and sweetness depending on their home climate and terrain.

Always cut 'em before takin' a bite, though. Just in case. —Zoë

Sadly, New Kasmir was one of the many outer worlds that became embroiled in the battle for independence against the Alliance. Although the skirmishes that took place here may not have done nearly as much permanent damage to the planet as those on Border worlds like Hera and Shadow, many lives were lost—often in unspeakably horrific ways—and the repercussions are still felt by all who dwell here. *And many who got the hell out. —Mal*

 ## SHOPPING AND ENTERTAINMENT

Grizwald's Apple Farm: There are dozens of popular orchards on New Kasmir that allow visitors to pick bushels of their own fresh fruit to take back home with them, but if you're looking for an added bonus, be sure to visit Grizwald's for a number of homemade apple products—including apple butter, apple jam, apple cider, applesauce, and, of course, Mama Grizwald's famous apple pie. It's guaranteed to blow your mind!

Now that's just tasteless. —Zoë

Pie lovers across the 'Verse seem to disagree. —Wash

WHITTIER

Whittier is one of many planets in the 'Verse whose culture is built around the plentiful waters on its surface and the creatures that dwell within them. Unlike New Melbourne, however, the majority of sea life on Whittier is spawned via highly controlled breeding programs.

Buckle up, kids! We're headed to the fish sex world! —Wash

HISTORY AND CULTURE

Whittier's shores are lined with enormous hatcheries that employ the majority of the populace. Within these fish farming factories, scientists carefully cultivate the most exotic aquatic creatures imaginable. These fish are raised in huge pens that stretch far out into the planet's seas until they are exported to other worlds across the 'Verse. As long as payment is made in full, Whittier's breeders don't care if their perfect specimens end up on display in an aquarium or on a plate in an expensive restaurant. *That I can respect. —Jayne*

DINING AND NIGHTLIFE

Flotsam: Many of the fish and other aquatic creatures bred on Whittier don't meet the high standards required for export and sale due to minor imperfections in their genetic makeup. While they may not be perfect, they still taste delicious, and Whittier's hottest restaurant, Flotsam, is proud to turn these rejects into delicacies. The menu changes nightly depending on availability, but the bistro's signature cloned caviar is always available and is guaranteed to be the perfect bite every time.

Kinda nice that even the rejects get their chance to shine, ain't it? —Kaylee

Genetic abnormalities don't exactly inspire my appetite. —Simon

BEYLIX

Easily recognizable by the icy rings that circle its center, Beylix is the first world orbiting the protostar Penglai and is beautiful to behold. Once on the surface of Beylix, though, you're likely to find yourself knee deep in rubbish, wishing that you'd just continued to admire it from afar.

I feel that way every time I exit my shuttle into the galley. —Inara

 ## HISTORY AND CULTURE

Beylix began, like most other Rim worlds, with a focus on farming and ranching. But it wasn't long before landowners were presented with lucrative contracts to convert their farmland into the Rim's first recycling centers. What they thought would help make the 'Verse a cleaner place made their planet a much filthier one, because a loophole in those contracts also allowed the planet to be used for the permanent storage of nonrecyclable refuse, essentially turning Beylix into the 'Verse's only dedicated landfill planet.

While the hardworking people of Beylix continue to have pride in their home world despite its reputation as Kalidasa's trash bin, they have found themselves in increasingly dangerous circumstances as looters and scavengers flock to the world with delusions that they'll find their next big score buried somewhere beneath the endless piles of waste.

I'll grab the shovels. And the gloves. —JAYNE

 ## SHOPPING AND ENTERTAINMENT

Detonation Derby: It's become common for Beylix's younger settlers to salvage the remains of vehicles from the planet's scrapyards and customize them into powerful war machines for one of the planet's most dangerous forms of competition. These makeshift tanks collide with each other—often with explosive results thanks to the unstable ship parts they're retrofitted with—until only one is left functioning and a champion is crowned.

Ooh! Captain! Can I borrow the mule? PLEEEEASE?!? —Kaylee

NEWHALL

Yet another watery world, Newhall is the second planet orbiting Penglai. Newhall's vast oceans created some unique challenges for its settlers early on, but they have since managed to turn the tides in their favor.

 ## HISTORY AND CULTURE

Settlers may have come to Newhall to answer the call of the open seas, but as they made homes on the plentiful island chains, they soon discovered a major flaw in their new world. While there was more salt water than they could ever need, fresh water was exceptionally scarce. The construction of massive desalination plants not only provided the citizens of Newhall with the means to survive, it also changed their culture in an unexpected way.

First and foremost, the nearly endless supply of water on Newhall can be processed and exported to planets with naturally dry conditions to be used for drinking, crop irrigation, and manufacturing. In addition, the highly concentrated salt brine, which is a by-product of the desalination process has become a valuable export, used for preserving vegetables and curing meats on Border and Rim worlds. *Hijacked an entire tanker of this stuff once. —Mal*

Got us in quite the pickle. —Wash

 ## SHOPPING AND ENTERTAINMENT

Severance Saltwater Sweets: Located on Newhall's first moon, Severance, what started as a small handmade-candy shop has expanded to become a 'Verse-wide favorite thanks to affordable prices and an exciting assortment of flavors. There isn't a fair or bazaar in the system that doesn't have a licensed SSS vendor selling the company's tantalizing treats by the handful. Their signature taffy is well worth the teeth you're likely to lose chewing it.

And they likely make a fortune melting down the fillings lost by the poor idiots who chew this lè sè. —Inara

My favorite's the strawberry. —JAYNE

OBERON

Penglai's third world, Oberon, is currently uninhabitable. It is scheduled for terraforming along with its three moons, Puck, Quince, and Bottom.

HISTORY AND CULTURE

While Beylix and Newhall may have traveled their own distinct paths to civilization, none can argue their significance to the modern day Kalidasa system. As such, Penglai's visitors often question why it has taken so long to terraform the third world in the system, Oberon. The answer is quite simple: Oberon was originally scheduled to be terraformed alongside its fellow Penglai worlds in 2425. Unfortunately, a rogue asteroid from the large swarm on Penglai's outer orbit broke loose and hit Oberon, wiping out the terraforming crew and all of their progress. Crews turned their attention to other planets and moons in the Rim while they waited for Oberon's conditions to stabilize enough for another attempt.

Oberon is now scheduled to be habitable by 2560, with its moons following shortly after.

Another asteroid could hit at any time. Why would anyone willingly put themselves at such risk? —Simon

BEEN WONDERIN' THE SAME THING SINCE YOU AND YOUR SISTER CAME ABOARD. —JAYNE

123

GHOST

Not yet terraformed, the planet called Ghost circles Kalidasa in its twelfth orbital path. It is the last of the five uninhabitable worlds in the Kalidasa system and is scheduled for terraforming along with its moons, Inferno and Xibalia.

 ## HISTORY AND CULTURE

The first planet beyond Penglai, Ghost earned its name thanks to a strange phenomenon. For decades, travelers who pass by this solitary world have picked up "ghost signals" on their comm equipment that seem to come directly from the planet's surface. Upon scanning, no traces of life are found. Alliance scientists have determined that the planet's crust is primarily made of granite, limestone, and magnetite, all elements known to have the ability to retain electrical imprints. It is theorized that these signals are actually residual traces of signals broadcast by ships that passed near Ghost years before. Of course that hasn't stopped countless curious explorers from searching this lifeless world for traces of something more sinister.

Ghost is scheduled to be habitable by 2545, with its moons following shortly after.

If you happen to pick up a broadcast with coordinates for buried treasure on Xibalia, it's totally not part of an elaborate prank! Really! I swear! —Wash

ABERDEEN

Sihnon may be considered the fashion capital of the 'Verse, but beyond the Core, most folks don't care much about *haute couture*. To survive out on the edge of space, durability and comfort are key—and when it comes to those, nothing beats the clothing made on Aberdeen.

 ## HISTORY AND CULTURE

It's easy to dismiss Aberdeen as yet another standard farm and factory world, but this planet's importance can be witnessed in every closet from the Core to the Rim. Unlike other worlds that farm their crops and raise their livestock strictly as food, Aberdeen has evolved in a different direction, growing endless fields of cotton and raising sheep for wool. Once harvested, these raw materials are taken to textile mills and woven into strong garments well suited for life in the 'Verse's more rugged regions.

My rugged regions could always use a tad more comfort. —Jayne

 ## TIPS FOR A FUN TRIP

DO: Try something new. It's common for frequent travelers to get stuck in their ways when it comes to clothing, wearing the same outfit over and over for the sake of convenience. Adding a new piece to your regular wardrobe—like a vest, a belt, or a long coat—can give your signature look a bit of extra flare for a reasonable price.

Perhaps it's time you considered a new coat, Mal... —Inara

This one's seen less action than your bed, woman, and you don't hear me tellin' you to change your mattress. —Mal

DON'T: Try the mutton. Despite their abundance, sheep are treated with the utmost dignity and respect on Aberdeen and are not used as a food source except in emergencies. Farmers protect their herds with the same devotion as they would their own families.

ZEUS

The smallest of the 'Verse's gas giants, Zeus travels around Kalidasa in the system's fourteenth orbit. Though Zeus itself may not be habitable, the settlements on its moons have learned to thrive around a planet that many feared could not be tamed.

Maybe we can find a way to live with River after all . . . —Jayne

 ## HISTORY AND CULTURE

Like the mythological god for which it is named, Zeus is a truly majestic presence in the heavens. It may not be as large as some of the other gas giants in the 'Verse, but the violently swirling storms that cover its surface have been raging for centuries with no end in sight. Zeus's weather patterns are so volatile that they occasionally create cosmic disturbances that can be felt on the nearby moons. For that reason, the moons of Zeus were originally disqualified for terraforming.

I've been disqualified for just about everything other than my pilot's license. Never stopped me either. —Wash

A group of scientists petitioned the Alliance, claiming that proximity to Zeus would allow them to study the planet's weather patterns in ways that could help them better understand and control natural phenomena on other habitable worlds in the 'Verse. Their research has led to major breakthroughs in atmo stabilization on multiple planets and is being integrated into the terraforming process for many new worlds scheduled for colonization.

? DID YOU KNOW?:

· Five of Zeus's six moons are terraformed. The first moon, Isabel, has the smallest population of the five habitable satellites. It is primarily used as a station for powerful planetary scanning equipment.

· Zeus's outermost moon, Betty, is currently scheduled for terraforming due to the expansion of the atmo research team.

· Ninety percent of the power used by the colonies on these moons is drawn directly from the electromagnetic energy released into the black by Zeus's powerful planet-wide storms.

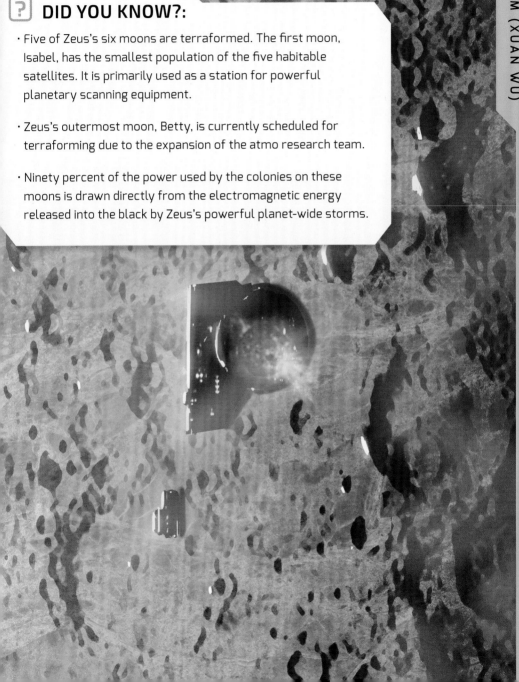

BEAUMONDE

Close to the edge of the Kalidasa system sits Beaumonde, perhaps the most prominent industrial world in the 'Verse. If you're traveling the system looking for work, Beaumonde gladly welcomes anyone who's willing to get their hands—and their lungs—a little dirty. *Don't mind gettin' a little filthy as long as it ends with us gettin' filthy rich. —Mal*

 ## HISTORY AND CULTURE

One would assume that Beaumonde, with a name that means "beautiful world," would closely rival the splendor of Sihnon. Sadly, such is not the case. Instead, the seventeenth planet in the Kalidasa system is a center of industry that becomes more polluted every day. Great factories that produce everything from catalyzers to Cortex consoles spew their smoke into the sky, creating a murky haze that makes it virtually impossible to see some of the planet's sprawling cities from space. *Hell, you can barely see them when you're standing right in the middle of them. —Zoë*

There was likely a time when Beaumonde lived up to its moniker, however, a fact still evidenced by patches of serene farmland that exist beyond the noxious air spreading from the major metropolises that serve as the planet's main manufacturing centers.

One can only imagine that the unchecked spread of airborne contaminants on Beaumonde could lead the planet toward a fate not dissimilar to that which befell Earth-That-Was generations ago. Fortunately, all of Beaumonde's industrial leaders have signed the Dazhong Accords, an agreement to help reverse the negative effects that pollutants are having on the planet's climate and environment.

The agreement is still tentative and there is fear that some may pull out. —Inara

Bet that's not somethin' you usually have to worry about. —Mal

GETTING AROUND

Flying isn't easy in the industrial areas of Beaumonde, due to the thick layer of smog that hangs in the air. You can try to stay below the cloud line, but you'll be dodging smokestacks from the factories below. Your best option is to dock your ship in one of the planet's rural regions and travel into the polluted zones on land.

I learned to fly in polluted skies. It just takes a little extra concentration. —Wash

And an assortment of extra prayers. —Book

WHAT TO WEAR

Beaumonde is strictly a working class planet, so there's no need to fancy up before coming here. However, it might be wise to bring a breathing mask and some spare oxygen if you're planning on visiting any of the city centers. The settlers here have somehow adjusted to breathing in the toxic fumes, but tourists rarely even make it a few hours before their lungs start to feel the impact of the adulterated atmo.

I LIKE A bit of burnin'. Reminds me that I'm still alive. —JAYNE

DINING AND NIGHTLIFE

Maidenhead: If you're docked on Beaumonde, be sure to head on down to one of the planet's most exclusive underground clubs, Maidenhead. Anyone with fantasies of living like a crime lord will feel at home in this cavern-turned-bar, complete with fan dancers, hookah pipes, and a big screen hanging over the bar. Table service is available for those who want a bit of extra privacy when conducting "business" with some of the establishment's more notorious regulars. Security is high here, so be sure to check any personal weapons in the provided storage lockers and make sure your drinking buddies are on their best behavior.

Ask for Fanty and Mingo . . . then try to figure out which one is which. —Zoë

DJINN'S BANE

The largest of the three gas giants in the Kalidasa system, Djinn's Bane is far calmer than Zeus, allowing settlers on its moons to take advantages of this vaporous world's plentiful—and highly coveted—resources.

 ## HISTORY AND CULTURE

Anyone looking to use this book to chart their course across the 'Verse knows the importance of loading up on fuel before a long journey. Most ships run on hydrogen-based fuels, and there's no better source for pure hydrogen than a gas giant. Thankfully, the brave citizens inhabiting the moons around Djinn's Bane have made it possible for us to top off our tanks without ever putting our own lives at risk. *Clearly written by someone who's never had to steal fuel before. —Mal*

The first two moons orbiting Djinn's Bane—Illat and Hilal—are used as launching points for extraction crews, as well as equipment maintenance and storage. The next three moons—Hubal, Sin, and Ta' Lab—contain the facilities that process the hydrogen for various uses and ship it across the 'Verse. Finally, the last moon of Djinn's Bane—Wadd—acts as the Rim's most popular service station. You simply can't beat the prices on fuel found here!

Once again, written by someone who's never stolen fuel before. —Wash

 ## LODGING

Djinn's Inn: If you're already stopping near Djinn's Bane to fill up your ship, you might as well fill up your belly and rest your head. The Djinn's Inn travel lodge is located on the fourth moon of Djinn's Bane, Sin. Despite this moon's sultry name, the only thing sinful to be found at this no-frills motel is the homemade pie served at the adjoining diner. Rooms, on the other hand, are significantly less extravagant, containing little more than a bed, a bathroom, and a view of the nearby refinery. But since you chose to come this far out on the Rim, you probably weren't looking for a five-star resort anyway.

Yet this is, perhaps, the only night of Sin you could convince me to partake in. —Book

SALISBURY

The final planet in the Kalidasa system, Salisbury was originally slated to be one of the most advanced worlds on the Rim. Sadly, this small world has since become known throughout the 'Verse for all the wrong reasons.

I know the feeling. —Simon

 ## HISTORY AND CULTURE

During a period in its rotation when Salisbury was closest to the Border, the Alliance chose this world to become the home of the Rim's most sophisticated medical facilities, providing the same kind of care one might find in the Core to the settlers on the edge of the black. Unfortunately, mismanagement of funds by a greedy governor led to a total collapse of infrastructure, and the hospitals were never completed.

Even though construction was suddenly halted, shipments of valuable medical supplies—including endless cases of potent pharmaceuticals—were already en route from Ariel and Greenleaf. Upon delivery, the provisions were seized by Salisbury's disenfranchised settlers, who then used them to create a new stream of revenue by selling them to the highest bidders. Once the meds ran dry, the settlers found themselves not only without a way to make a living, but also plagued with addiction from consuming a large portion of the supplies themselves.

AMATEURS. EVERYONE KNOWS YOU DON'T SAMPLE THE GOODS! —JAYNE

 ## TIPS FOR A FUN TRIP

DO: Offer a hand. Salisbury has also become a popular stop for missionaries and aid workers from the Core who hope to help the impoverished settlers overcome their addictions.

Comforting to know that there is still good in the 'Verse, even out here. —Book

DON'T: Offer a hit. Many of the settlers on Salisbury are genuinely devoted to breaking their cycle of dependency. You might be able to make easy credits here selling stolen meds, but your actions could destroy years of personal progress.

LI SHEN'S BAZAAR

If you're tired of drifting through the black and are in dire need of an interesting diversion, look no further than Li Shen's Bazaar, a floating port station packed full of unique foods, interesting sights, and helpful services to help get your adventure back on track.

 ## HISTORY AND CULTURE

If the journey between planets is taking its toll on you or your crew, it might be time to make a quick pit stop to refuel, stretch your legs, and stock up on supplies. There are hundreds of orbiting outposts scattered throughout the systems of the 'Verse, but none have a wider variety of goods—and bads—than Li Shen's Bazaar. *Good lord, I love this crazy place. —Wash*

The interior of this self-contained spaceport is one of the most eclectic marketplaces you'll ever experience. Billboards flash in bright colors as barkers beckon visitors to experience the lost wonders of the 'Verse. Strange smells waft from every stall, many of them strangely enticing.

Most of them extremely revolting. —Inara

While it may seem like a tourist trap on the surface, this floating city was actually designed to accommodate the needs of busy crews on the go. The branches of the Allied Postal System and St. Lucy's Medical Center on the station mean that those who don't have a planet to call their own always have a home base they can return to between missions. *Just be sure never to accept a package without checkin' what's inside first. —Mal*

ETIQUETTE

Like any orbital station, Li Shen's Bazaar has thousands of people from different areas of the 'Verse pass through it every day. When customs from so many different worlds are represented, it can be hard to know which ones should get priority. Show respect and basic decency to those around you and you should get the same in return. *OR THROW A RANDOM PUNCH AND WATCH CHAOS ERUPT. —JAYNE*

 ## SHOPPING AND ENTERTAINMENT

The Bazaar of the Bizarre: A small stretch of Li Shen's has become known for the display of rarities and oddities found at the far reaches of the 'Verse. Though there are some genuine relics from Earth-That-Was on display that are worth the price of admission, other attractions—such as the supposed remains of an alien creature—are a bit more questionable. *It was just a cow fetus. —Simon*
Didn't make it any less bizarre. ~Kaylee

DINING AND NIGHTLIFE

While there are hundreds of strange things to eat in the Bazaar's market district, no single dining destination stands out more than the others. If you are an adventurous eater, try as many items from as many vendors as you can. With fish tacos you'd swear were straight from New Melbourne and ice planets nearly as cold as St. Albans itself, you're in for some real treats.

➡ TIPS FOR A FUN TRIP

DO: Bring your wallet. The merchants in the Bazaar deal in a wide variety of unique items from planets that you might not ever have the chance to visit. Shopkeepers here are unlikely willing to accept electronic credits, so be sure to have a little extra cash in hand in order to make a few impulse purchases.

DON'T: Lose your wallet. The narrow laneways and bustling crowds of the Bazaar are unfortunately the perfect place for pickpockets to practice their skills, so keep your money in a safe place on your person at all times. Of course, you could be just as easily robbed by purchasing a garment made of "authentic" Sihnon silk only to find that it is a cottony counterfeit. *Oh, the horror! —Wash*

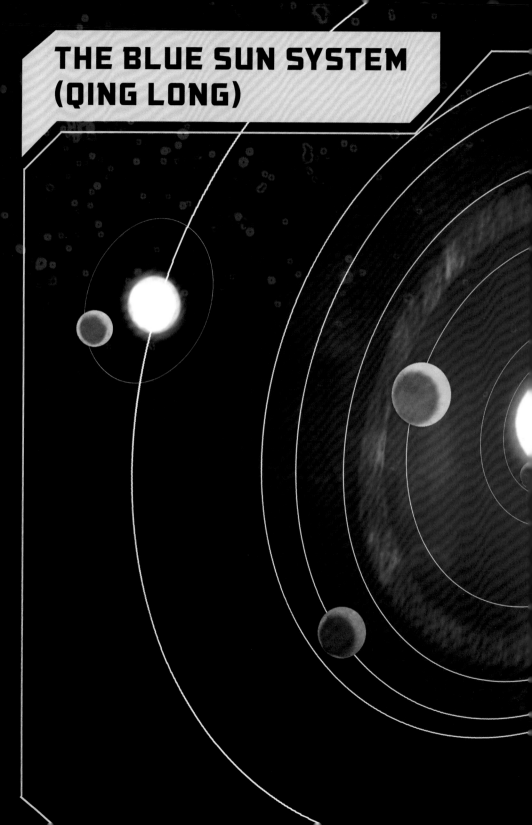

THE BLUE SUN SYSTEM (QING LONG)

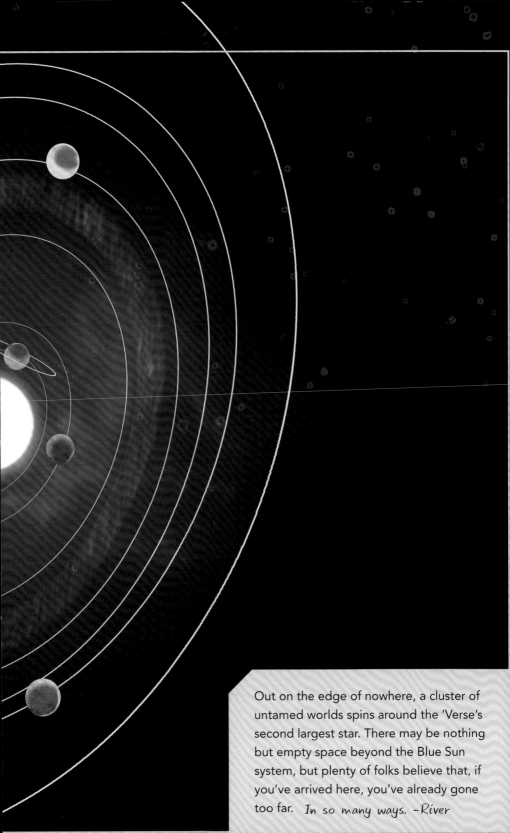

Out on the edge of nowhere, a cluster of untamed worlds spins around the 'Verse's second largest star. There may be nothing but empty space beyond the Blue Sun system, but plenty of folks believe that, if you've arrived here, you've already gone too far. *In so many ways. —River*

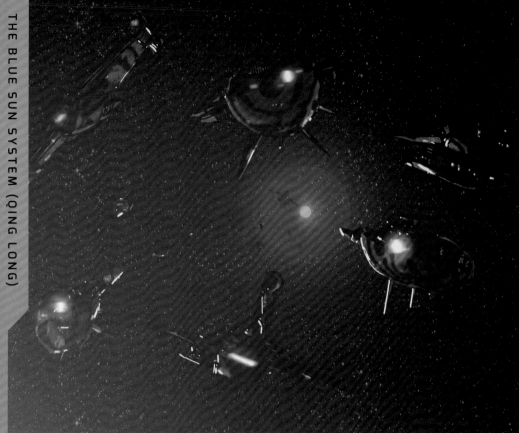

🏛 HISTORY AND CULTURE

Situated in the final path orbiting Bai Hu, Qing Long is a bright blue star that illuminates the last traces of human civilization. Whereas most Core worlds have populations that number in the billions, the entire Blue Sun system combined is only home to several million settlers—scarcely enough to populate some Border moons. *My home city on Sihnon had more citizens than this entire system. —Inara*

Remind me never to visit there. —Mal

You weren't invited. —Inara

There are certainly logical reasons for the decreased number of citizens in the Blue Sun system. The system's distance from the rest of the 'Verse has affected everything from Alliance law enforcement presence to the availability of basic supplies. This level of isolation can be a blessing or a curse depending on who you ask, but everyone can agree on one thing: Out here, every settler truly has to fend for themselves.

Fortunately, that's somethin' we've become accustomed to. —Zoë

Speak for yourselves. —Simon

That means the kind of folks you find on Blue Sun planets are willing to do whatever it takes to survive. For some, that means hiding out on worlds where no one will ever look for them. For others, it means taking whatever they want from those around them with little fear of consequence. Either way, it's fair to assume that nearly all of the settlers who call the Blue Sun system home only came here as a last resort. We suggest you do the same.

Well, that's a mite harsh for a vacation guide, now ain't it? —Jayne

 ## TIPS FOR A FUN TRIP

DO: Cross through Uroborus. On the interior of the Blue Sun system's asteroid belt, you'll find some of the more civilized planets in the system, including Meridian and New Canaan. Just be sure to steer clear of the prison moons of Fury!

DON'T: Cross into Reaver Space. Although Reavers occasionally travel closer to the Border, the highest concentration of these notoriously savage space pirates is in the Blue Sun system. Reavers tend to congregate in large fleets, particularly on the outer edge of the system near the protostar Burnham. Avoid this region at all cost, unless being skinned and eaten alive is your idea of a fun vacation.

I bet there are some Reavers reading this who just got very excited . . . . – Wash

? DID YOU KNOW?

· The name "Qing Long" means "blue dragon," an ancient Chinese symbol representing the east and the element wood.

· The planets in the Blue Sun system have orbital paths that run perpendicular to those in the 'Verse's other major systems.

· The protostar Burnham is a helioformed brown dwarf that travels in the Blue Sun's final orbital path. It is orbited by ~~the planet Miranda~~ **NO HABITABLE PLANETS.**

Well, that ain't the slightest bit suspicious, now is it? —Mal

MERIDIAN

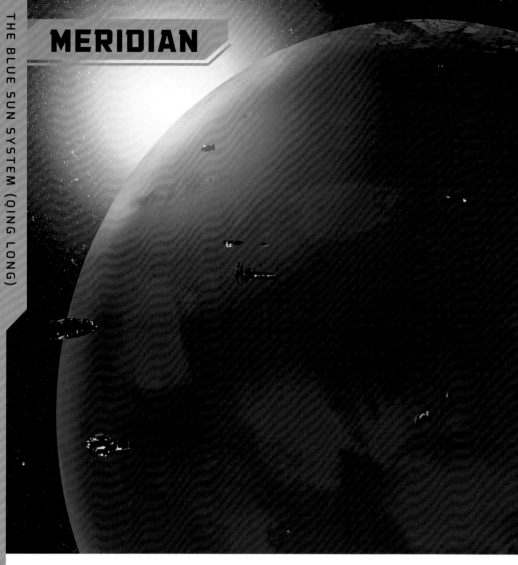

The Blue Sun's first planet, Meridian, boasts the highest population of any of its worlds. Thanks to the presence of a major conglomerate, Meridian may be the closest thing you'll find to a Core world this far out on the Rim.

 HISTORY AND CULTURE *That ain't exactly a resoundin' recommendation. —Mal*

The Blue Sun system's capital, Meridian, is the headquarters for the Blue Sun Corporation, one of the 'Verse's most prolific and influential manufacturers of goods in every category. Although their products are sold on every planet, the company deliberately chose a world on the outer Rim of the 'Verse for their center of operations in order to protect valuable trade secrets.

God forbid someone unlock the dark secrets of the Fruity Oaty Bar! —Wash

The corporation pumps a steady flow of credits into its home world, allowing its employees to continue living the comfortable lives they abandoned when they moved to the Rim to join the staff. Meridian's city centers feature many of the modern conveniences found on most Core planets, including a mass transit system and high-speed Cortex feeds. The planet also has heightened protection from potential thieves and raiders, thanks to Blue Sun's own personal security team.

Best thing about paid security? You can always pay 'em more to look the other way. —Zoë

SHOPPING AND ENTERTAINMENT

Blue Sun Company Stores: Blue Sun products are in every store in the 'Verse, but employees of the Blue Sun Corporation have access to a chain of outlets on Meridian that sell the company's products—from foodstuffs to tech gear—at deep discounts. Though the heavily reduced prices are usually reserved for Blue Sun staff members, the store has a semiannual "friends and family" sale that expands the markdowns to the general populace. Sale weekends have been known to draw in more shoppers from across the 'Verse than there are settlers on Meridian.

They sell Blue Sun Cola by the barrel! Who needs fresh water when we could have unlimited liquid caffeine? –Kaylee

THAT EXPLAINS SOME THINGS . . . —JAYNE

NEW CANAAN

The second planet in the Blue Sun system may be the system's most frequently visited due to its inclusion as part of an important shipping circuit. Far more civilized than some of its fellow Rim worlds, New Canaan offers some of the comforts of home on the edge of the 'Verse.

 ## HISTORY AND CULTURE

Every system in the 'Verse has a planet that serves as a central point for trade and commerce. For the Blue Sun system, that planet is New Canaan. While the spaceports on New Canaan may not be nearly as busy as their counterparts on Persephone, they still accommodate the majority of crucial imports and exports for all worlds on this side of the Border. That means New Canaan sees a lot of crews come and go each day—and this far out on the Rim, danger hides around every asteroid, so the faster they can go, the better!

That's why Serenity is ready to go full burn at any moment. —Kaylee

And even that isn't always fast enough out here. —Wash

While the Alliance may not choose to allocate personnel to enforce the law on every Rim planet, they are willing to pay a handsome sum to contracted security firms. While those efforts are more abundant on planets like New Canaan that are of greater economic interest to the Alliance, even small moons like Lilac see the benefit of this practice in terms of general safety and job creation.

Fortunately, New Canaan's docks aren't nearly as regulated as the ports closer to the Core. That means ships can arrive and depart as they please, often without having to go through the proper customs procedures. That makes it easy for crews to land, unload, reload, and go with minimal hassle.

Or even pick up undocumented cargo that wouldn't be so easy to slip off more heavily monitored worlds. —Zoë

Not that anyone would condone such behavior. —Book

Keep tellin' yourself that, Shepherd. —Zoë

 DINING AND NIGHTLIFE

Port & Sherry: New Canaan is home to a number of distilleries, providing the 'Verse with some of its finest aged spirits. A popular nightspot for traders weary from their long voyage to the Rim, Port & Sherry has bartenders who fill snifters with libations straight from the barrel—including a rare eighty-year-old New Canaan brandy that fetches nearly two thousand credits a bottle on some Core worlds. As its name suggests, Port & Sherry is conveniently located close to the spaceport so that crews can stumble home after enjoying one glass too many.

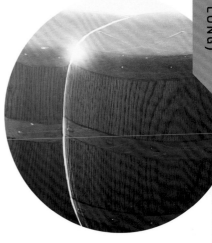

 TIPS FOR A FUN TRIP

DO: Enjoy a good run. The planet lends its name to one of the most popular commercial trade routes in the 'Verse, the New Canaan Run. While New Canaan may be just one of eleven planets on this nearly sixty-week journey, it is the furthest destination on the Rim before ships turn back toward the Core.

DON'T: Get too comfortable! Because of its location on the Rim, its importance as a port planet, and its notorious lack of Alliance presence, New Canaan is a frequent target for thieves and scoundrels. New Canaan and its moons have even been known to be unexpectedly raided by bloodthirsty Reavers, so be prepared to flee at a moment's notice. Your life may depend on it.

Reavers show up, ain't time to play hero. You save yourself and your crew. Everyone else is on their own. —Mal

Good thing that we're on the crew then, I suppose. —Simon

Did we ever actually make that official? —Mal

MUIR

The third planet in the Blue Sun system, Muir is known for the production of weapons used throughout the 'Verse, from basic revolvers to powerful auto-cannons. If you're in need of a little extra firepower, Muir will guarantee that you're fully loaded.   *You can just drop me off here. —Jayne*

 ## HISTORY AND CULTURE

While the Blue Sun Corporation has dipped into virtually every viable market in the 'Verse, one area that the commerce giant rarely dabbles in—at least publically—is the production of weapons. The Callahan Company filled that void, setting up shop on Muir to manufacture a wide variety of armaments for a system in dire need of personal protection. Their expert craftsmen have produced some of the most respected firearms in the 'Verse, including the legendary Callahan full-bore auto-lock rifle.   *Her name is Vera. —Jayne*

The people of Muir have a strategic partnership with the nearby moons of Fury, providing artillery for the security guards stationed at their prisons. In exchange, Callahan participates in a work-release program that provides the company unpaid labor from Fury's inmates.

Allowing prisoners access to guns seems like a poor choice. —Simon

I would take them over Jayne any day. —River

 ## SIGHTS AND ACTIVITIES

Shepherd's Mission: The second moon of Muir is home to a number of abbeys and monasteries focused on delivering a message of peace to the furthest reaches of the 'Verse. Because of the moon's proximity to the weapons factories on the planet below, Shepherd's Mission hosts an ongoing peaceful protest—now in its fiftieth year—to promote an end to unnecessary violence. Visitors are always welcome on Shepherd's Mission and are encouraged to participate.

It's encouraging to see so many standing against these weapons of war. —Book

IF THEY STAND STILL ENOUGH, I MIGHT BE ABLE TO TAKE SOME OF 'EM OUT FROM MUIR. —JAYNE

FURY

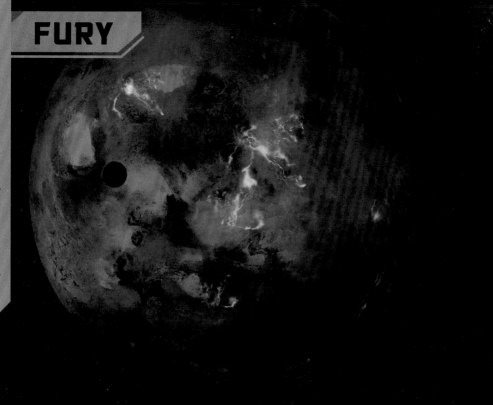

The largest gas giant in the entire 'Verse, Fury's diameter is even larger than that of a protostar. Though the planet itself is not habitable, its two terraformed moons are used as maximum security prisons for some of the 'Verse's most ruthless criminals.

 ## HISTORY AND CULTURE

Like all gas giants, Fury could not be terraformed due to a lack of an accessible solid surface. Even if it could support life, however, Fury's unpredictable atmo is constantly erupting in electrical fluctuations that make the storms on Zeus look tame. Most travelers avoid Fury, making two of its small moons, Coldstone and Blackwood, perfect locations to hold vicious criminals who would pose constant danger on more civilized worlds.

Both of the prison complexes on Fury's moons are run by an independent security company that is under contract with the Alliance. Coldstone serves as the general population prison for offenders who show a chance of rehabilitation, while Blackwood is reserved for violent repeat offenders with a lower likelihood of reintegration into society. We may not be the most law-abidin' folks in the 'Verse, but ain't none of us ever done nothin' worthy of landin' here. —Mal

Are you trying to convince us or yourself? —Inara

Fury's third moon, Seventh Circle, is currently scheduled to be terraformed and is slated to serve as a solitary confinement facility.

 ## LODGING

Since the prisons on Fury's moons are run by a for-profit company, unoccupied cells are available for rent at an extremely low rate. That doesn't mean we recommend using them. The cells aren't much larger than a standard berth on a passenger ship, the amenities are nonexistent, and the chances of being caught up in a riot are fairly high. But if you absolutely need to get off your ship for a while and don't have an abundance of credits to spare, renting a vacant cell might be one of the safer options in the Blue Sun system.

I'm perfectly fine sleeping directly below the highly radioactive ship engine, thank you very much. —Simon

HIGHGATE

The fifth planet in the Blue Sun system, Highgate was originally envisioned as the most modern world in the system, but when its cities were seized by warring criminal factions, those dreams vanished, and Highgate was left to fester in its own corruption.

HISTORY AND CULTURE

Highgate was the first planet intended to serve as the capital of the Blue Sun system, with the Alliance investing billions of credits into the construction of cities and infrastructure. Unfortunately, those projects would never see completion.

Like many planets on the Rim, Highgate found itself populated by citizens who had no interest in universal law and order. Outlaws initially banded together to force out the Alliance, but they eventually turned against each other. The planet has since become a perpetual war zone, and the last vestiges of the Alliance's lofty plans for Highgate were bombed into oblivion long ago.

Dealin' with single crime lords is trouble enough. No use gettin' mixed up betwixt rivals. —Mal

ETIQUETTE

Pretty much anything you do or say on Highgate is likely to get you shot. Better just to pass by this planet and head to a more pleasant destination.

Like the prisons of Fury. —Zoë

 ## LODGING

Heart of Gold: Highgate's moon, Perth, is home to a pleasure house called Heart of Gold where you can spend the night with some of the sweetest young ladies in the Blue Sun system (for a fee, of course). These girls aren't registered Companions, which means they make their own rules and aren't afraid to enforce them. This brothel recently underwent a change in management after a disagreement with the local law, but what they're selling will always be in demand, so there's no sign of business slowing down.

Nandi would be proud of what she built here. —Inara

Helpin' those gals out earned us free visits for life. We should be damn proud, too! —Jayne

DRAGON'S EGG

The second gas giant in the Blue Sun system, Dragon's Egg is significantly smaller than Fury. The planet's five moons have very low populations, even for Rim worlds—but what they lack in humans, they more than make up for in other life-forms.

 ## HISTORY AND CULTURE

The moons of Dragon's Egg were originally part of a genetic exploration program cofunded by the Alliance and the Blue Sun Corporation to help populate Rim worlds with heartier strains of crops and livestock. Unfortunately, the program was shut down during the Unification War due to a reallocation in funding.

Leave it to the Alliance to run away even when they win. —Mal

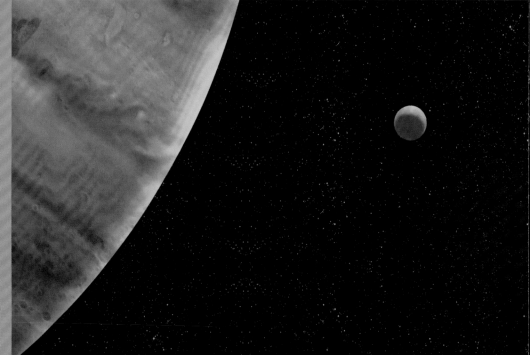

Despite the lack of official support, the scientists on these moons were dedicated to their mission and passionately continued their work. Without oversight from the Alliance, it is rumored that some of the experiments started to take darker turns, including the genetic manipulation of animal breeds and even human genomes. Those whispers only got louder when Dragon's Egg's outermost moon, Glynis, was permanently quarantined in 2510 with no attempt to evacuate its inhabitants.

SHOPPING AND ENTERTAINMENT

Dragon's Market: Located on Nakula, the third moon of Dragon's Egg, this is the only farmer's market in the 'Verse where everything is always in season. Not only can you restock your pantry with fresh fruits and veggies for long trips across the system, you can also taste test some of the unique hybrids being developed here—including the melutto, a surprisingly delicious prosciutto and melon crossbreed. Vendors from the adjacent moons also set up stands at the market, peddling livestock and adorable domesticated animals. You might question the ethics, but you definitely won't argue the prices!

Three words: Black. Market. Beagles. —Wash

DEADWOOD

Deadwood was a planet that faced adversity from its earliest days, but settlers took what could have easily been classified as a blackrock and turned it into a viable world. A visit to Deadwood gives a glimpse at how settlers on the Rim are often able to make the best out of the worst.

 ## HISTORY AND CULTURE

The seventh planet in the Blue Sun system, Deadwood began its life as a lush forest planet with plenty of promise for colonists looking to carve their own path on a new home far from the Core. Due to a quirk in the terraforming process, however, the soil on Deadwood was not able to maintain the proper level of nutrients to sustain vegetation for long. By the time colonists arrived, the forests had already begun to wither and die, leaving behind tall spires of barren wood that gave the planet its name.

"The Blue Sun system: Even our forests die unexpectedly." –Wash

Unable to produce crops in the planet's substandard soil, settlers considered abandoning Deadwood altogether. However, it was soon discovered that many of the vital minerals missing from Deadwood's dirt could be mined on the planet's two moons, Haven and New Omaha. Now, Deadwood and its moons share a symbiotic relationship, with the moons enhancing the soil and the planet providing them fresh crops in return.

I've discovered that the most unusual relationships can often become the most beneficial. –Inara

The large swaths of infertile forest are not completely wasted either, as savvy entrepreneurs bought up sections of the land as timber farms. Once the giant trees are cut down, they are treated to prevent any further decay, carved into beams and posts, and shipped to nearby worlds to be used in the construction of homes and fences.

SIGHTS AND ACTIVITIES

Standing Timbers National Park: One of the largest noncommercial areas of forest on Deadwood has been protected from deforestation by the planet's governing system. It serves as a reminder of the planet's earliest struggles and a monument to the settlers who overcame it. A gift shop at the entrance of the park offers souvenir "Deadwood Forests," which are popular with young visitors, though you could easily make your own at home for half the price with a pot of dirt and a few small twigs. *I bought two! —Wash* *Wouldn't expect any less. —Zoë*

[?] DID YOU KNOW?

· One of Deadwood's two moons, Haven, was established as a mining colony but has since become a sanctuary for those looking to make amends for their past crimes.

· Ships on the run from the law have been rumored to use Haven's network of mining shafts to avoid attention from Alliance operatives, so be wary before exploring any tunnels.

· Though some of Haven's inhabitants may still be smugglers at heart, it is said that most have found peace at the edge of the 'Verse and are trying to reform. *I think I'd like to pay this Haven a visit someday. —Book*

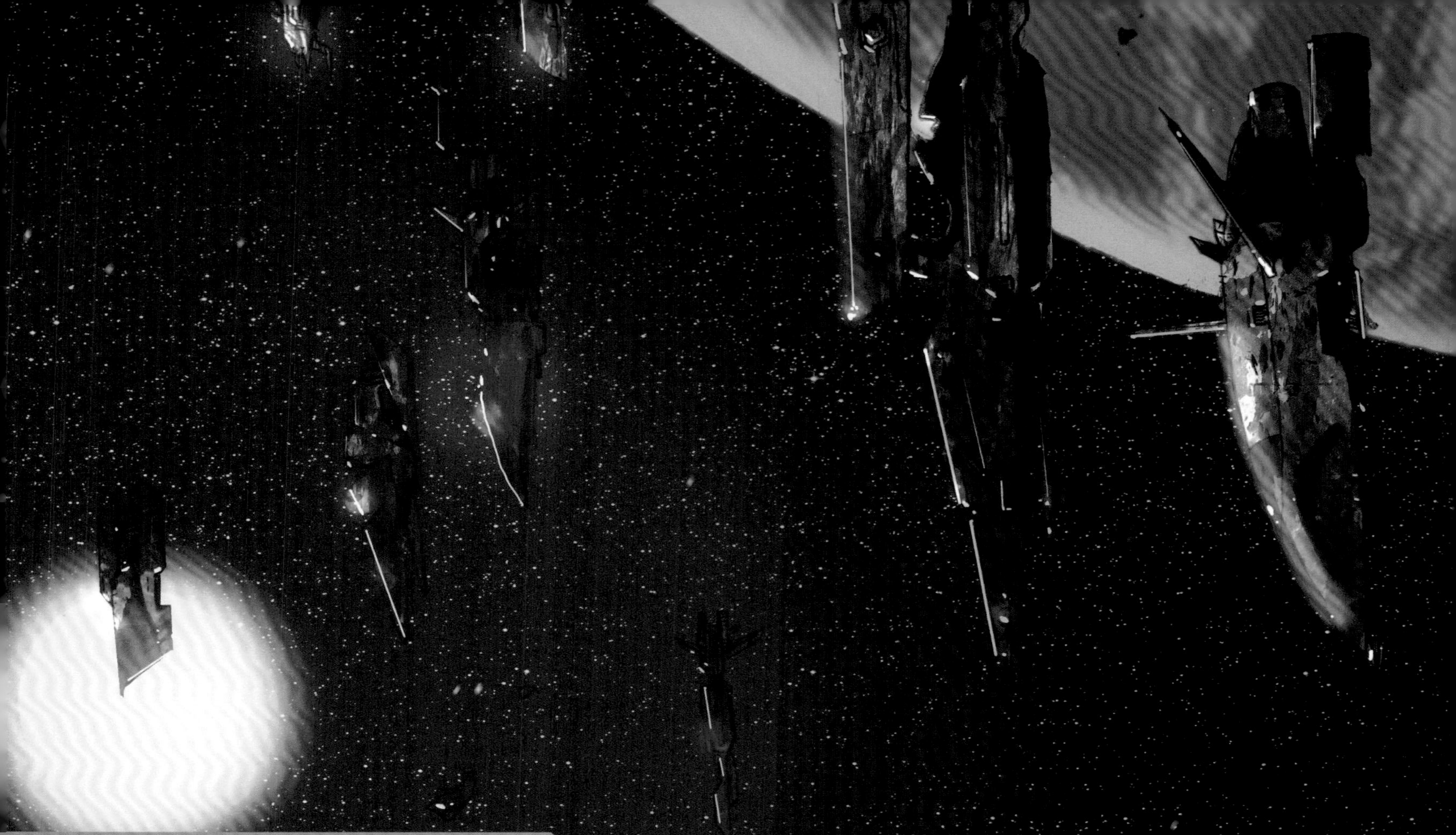

THE BLUE SUN SYSTEM (QING LONG)

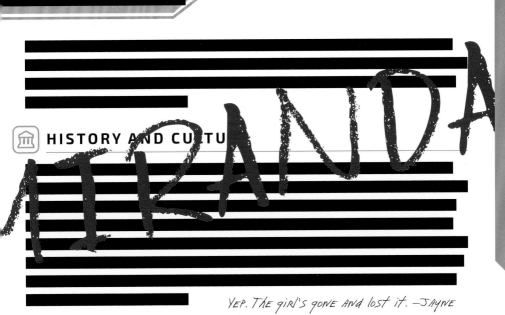

🏛 **HISTORY AND CULTU**

MIRANDA

Yep. The girl's gone and lost it. —JAYNE

AFTERWORD

A captain once told me a story.

He said he had traveled from one end of this 'Verse to the other, yet somehow he still did not believe in God. Shocked, I asked him what he had seen in his travels.

He told me of gleaming cities that touched the clouds and dusty mines that stretched deep beneath the ground. He told me of bounty that could fill a billion bellies and famine that could bring a world to its knees. He told me of grave injustices by those with power and great sacrifices by those without.

And he told me of people he encountered—their happiness and their suffering, their prosperity and their poverty, their love and their heartache. He told me of their ability to overcome even the greatest odds and survive on worlds where they were never meant to exist, fighting for the barren rocks that they called home.

Man, he said, had done all of this without the help of my God. And he seemed to believe it.

So I asked him to take me with him. To show me what he had seen so that I could witness it with my own eyes. And our journeys showed me more than I could have dreamed—the greatest joys and the deepest sorrows the 'Verse could offer. And my faith was only strengthened.

The captain may not yet see God in all of these beautiful worlds silently spinning through the black. But I do. And I will be glad to continue on this journey until we finally find him . . . together.

Shepherd Derrial Book

INSIGHT EDITIONS

PO Box 3088
San Rafael, CA 94912
www.insighteditions.com

 Find us on Facebook: www.facebook.com/InsightEditions

Follow us on Twitter: @insighteditions

Library of Congress Cataloging-in-Publication Data available.

ISBN: 978-1-68383-064-1

Publisher: Raoul Goff
Associate Publisher: Vanessa Lopez
Art Director: Chrissy Kwasnik
Designer: Evelyn Furuta
Editor: Paul Ruditis
Editorial Assistant: Tessa Murphy
Senior Production Editor: Elaine Ou
Production Managers: Sam Taylor and Jacob Frink

Illustrations by Livio Ramondelli

Insight Editions would like to thank Rossella Barry
for her help in the development of this book.

ROOTS of PEACE   REPLANTED PAPER

Insight Editions, in association with Roots of Peace, will plant two trees
for each tree used in the manufacturing of this book. Roots of Peace
is an internationally renowned humanitarian organization dedicated to
eradicating land mines worldwide and converting war-torn lands into
productive farms and wildlife habitats. Roots of Peace will plant two million
fruit and nut trees in Afghanistan and provide farmers there with the skills
and support necessary for sustainable land use.

Manufactured in China by Insight Editions

10 9 8 7 6 5 4 3 2 1